A Selection of Titles by Susan Rogers Cooper
available from Severn House

The E.J. Pugh Mysteries

ROMANCED TO DEATH
FULL CIRCLE
DEAD WEIGHT
GONE IN A FLASH
DEAD TO THE WORLD
STUDENT BODY

The Milt Kovak Series

SHOTGUN WEDDING
RUDE AWAKENING
HUSBAND AND WIVES
DARK WATERS
COUNTDOWN
BEST SERVED COLD

STUDENT BODY

STUDENT BODY

An E.J. Pugh Mystery

Susan Rogers Cooper

This first world edition published 2017
in Great Britain and the USA by
SEVERN HOUSE PUBLISHERS LTD of
19 Cedar Road, Sutton, Surrey, England, SM2 5DA.
Trade paperback edition first published
in Great Britain and the USA 2017 by
SEVERN HOUSE PUBLISHERS LTD

British Library Cataloguing in Publication Data
A CIP catalogue record for this title is available from the British Library.

ISBN-13: 978-0-7278-8711-5 (cased)
ISBN-13: 978-1-84751-819-4 (trade paper)
ISBN-13: 978-1-78010-883-4 (e-book)

All Severn House titles are printed on acid-free paper.

Severn House Publishers support the Forest Stewardship Council™ [FSC™],
the leading international forest certification organisation.
All our titles that are printed on FSC certified paper carry the FSC logo.

Typeset by Palimpsest Book Production Ltd.,
Falkirk, Stirlingshire, Scotland.
Printed and bound in Great Britain by
TJ International, Padstow, Cornwall.

ONE

Graham Pugh stood outside his dorm room door knowing two things: on the one hand, he was glad to be back from winter break; on the other, he was going to have to bite the bullet and kill his roommate.

There was just no way he could go another semester in the same room as Bishop 'Call Me Bish' Alexander. He was an arrogant asshole with a frat-boy mentality that no fraternity would let pledge. So Graham was stuck with him, day in and day out. He would admit, if only to himself, that Bishop was not a bad-*looking* guy: almost as tall as Graham, at least over six feet, with black hair and blue eyes that seemed to draw women like a magnet. But a broken magnet. None of them stayed more than a week.

Except Gretchen Morley. Gretchen was basically a female version of Bishop and, for the three weeks they were together, insisted the couple be dubbed 'Grebish.' Graham thought it sounded like a Kosher food item. No one ever, *ever* called them that. Maybe in a pique of self-loathing, Bishop had dumped Gretchen, something he'd never done with any other girl, to Graham's knowledge, and Gretchen, being the female equivalent of Bishop, keyed his car twice and sent him a box of Ex-Lax brownies. Bishop, to Graham's horror and delight, ate the entire lot. Graham moved into a friend's room for the duration of that particular incident.

But now, here he stood, contemplating murder. He knew a lot about murder, not from ever having committed one but from his mother's penchant for solving them. He wasn't so in awe of his mother for having this particular talent as he was in her ability to find so many dead bodies. *How many murdered people does the average human being know, for God's sake?* he often thought. But maybe she wouldn't get too involved in the murder of his roommate, being as how she was home in Black Cat Ridge and he was miles away in Austin at the

University of Texas. Surely, even if she did figure out he did it, she wouldn't turn him in. 'Right?' he asked himself. 'Maybe not?'

It was as he was contemplating these things that his dorm room door swung open and before him, in all his splendor, stood Bishop Alexander.

'Hey, Gray,' he said, shortening Graham's perfectly respectable name to Graham's continued annoyance. 'Didn't know you were back.'

'Yeah,' Graham said and pushed his way unceremoniously past his roommate.

'I was headed out,' Bishop said. 'Wanna come with?'

'No,' Graham said. Then, thinking that his mother really hadn't raised a total asshole, amended, 'Thanks, but I'm tired. Need to unpack and stuff.'

'Yeah, no doubt. Your mom send any goodies back with you?' Bishop asked.

Graham had one bag full of said goodies, but replied, 'Nope. Not this time.'

'Shit,' Bishop, whose own mother's idea of dinner was making reservations, said. 'See ya!' he called over his shoulder and was out the door.

And Graham sat down on his bed, head in hands, and thought, *Surely I can kill him and get away with it.*

Classes for the new semester started the next morning and he had a seven a.m. he hadn't been able to avoid. So he unpacked, made a quick dash to the dorm's cafeteria for a bite, then headed back to his room, read the syllabus for the seven a.m., checked to make sure he still had the right book and fell into bed. He was asleep in about two minutes – a feat he'd acquired at the age of thirteen but hadn't been able to pull off since he started college.

His alarm went off at six a.m. His eyes flew open and he wondered what the hell that noise was and why in the world anyone would want to wake up this early. Then he remembered his seven a.m. and struggled to a sitting position. He felt hungover but knew he hadn't had anything to drink the night before. *Damn early hour!* he thought. He had no idea what Bishop's schedule was and didn't really care. He made his way groggily to the bathroom, did his morning ritual and was headed to his desk to get his books when he saw the mess on the floor by Bishop's bed. His first reaction was: *Did the idiot not make it to the bathroom?* His second thought was: *Oh, shit, what did I do in my sleep?*

Today was my day to sleep in. Well, actually, every day was my day to sleep in lately. The girls – all three of them – were fairly self-sufficient, fixed their own breakfasts and took turns driving the old minivan to school. My husband, who never wanted to admit to a certain amount of self-sufficiency, had finally decided that if he wanted breakfast it was obvious he was going to have to make it himself. On this Monday morning the girls left early because of Megan's cheerleader practice, Alicia's band practice and Bess's need to find a nice quiet place to read. My three daughters – one by birth, one by adoption and one by fostering – were all either seventeen or about to be seventeen, and all three were seniors this year. Just the mere thought of the outlay of money that was ahead made my blood run cold. We were going to have four kids in college at the same time. The mind boggles.

My husband Willis was out the door that morning without breakfast by six-thirty due to an early meeting with a client. It was at a coffee shop so I wasn't terribly worried about his lack of calorific intake. I was asleep when the phone rang. Blissfully, soundly asleep.

Nothing lasts forever. Soundly was gone and blissfully might never return, I discovered upon answering the phone. 'What?' I growled.

'Mom! Oh, God, Mom! Help!'

I sat up in bed. 'Graham? What's wrong? What's happened? Are you OK?'

'It's Bishop, Mom. I think he's dead!' Graham said.

I took the phone away from my ear and looked at it. Maybe I was still asleep. Maybe I was dreaming all this. 'Graham?'

'Yeah, Mom?'

'Have you checked his pulse?' I asked.

'God, no! There's blood everywhere!' he said.

'Have you called the police?'

'Aw, well . . .'

'Graham!'

'Mom! I think maybe I did it. In my sleep,' he said, his voice almost a whisper. 'I've been wishing him dead, you know.'

That I *did* know. He'd mentioned it several times over the winter break, even once saying all he wanted for Christmas was Bishop's head on a platter, John the Baptist style.

'Graham, listen to me,' I said, using all my willpower to keep my voice calm and not start screaming. 'You need to call the police. Whatever you do, though, *do not* tell them you think you may have done it in your sleep. *Do not* tell them you wished him dead. Do you hear me?'

'Yes, ma'am.'

'What are you going to do?' I asked.

'Call the police,' he said.

'What are you going to tell them?'

'That he's dead?' he asked.

'Say you think something's wrong with your roommate. Say that you woke up and saw blood but you were afraid to touch him. Tell the nine-one-one operator to call the police and an ambulance.'

'OK,' my son said. 'But Mom?'

'What, honey?'

'What if—'

'What if nothing. Do what the police tell you to do and call me on my cell. Your dad and I are on our way.'

'OK. OK. Right,' he said and hung up without a goodbye. Under the circumstances, I decided not to hold that against him.

For once, it was a good thing Willis didn't get the contract with the man he'd met for breakfast that morning, because it wouldn't have done his reputation much good to cancel it immediately. I'd driven straight to his office to tell him about Graham's call in person. I'd already packed two bags and had them tucked in the small trunk of my two-seater Audi. After Willis had calmed down enough to be rational, we headed to the school to let the girls know we were going to Austin. We had to pull them all out of class and, as one unit, and in unison, they said, 'We're going with you!'

'We're in the Audi!' I said.

'We'll take the minivan!' Megan offered.

'The minivan won't make it to Austin. It will hardly make it to Codderville,' I said, mentioning the older town on the other side of the Texas Colorado River from our much newer town of Black Cat Ridge. The town where their grandmother, Willis's mother, lived and the only place to which, so far, the minivan had been able to make.

'We can go back and get my truck,' Willis said.

'Whatever,' I said. 'Let's just get on the road!'

So we checked the girls out of school, they ran home in the minivan to pack a quick bag (whenever Megan makes the claim of a quick anything, however, there is a universal rolling of eyes), and I followed them back in my Audi to secure it in the garage. Willis showed up in his entirely too big pickup truck that had room for all five of us – six if we needed to haul Graham around with us – and we headed west. Nothing is ever easy when you're dealing with six people, especially when three of them are teenaged girls.

It was one of those perfect winter days we often get in south central Texas. The sun was shining, the temperature was in the high seventies by noon and sweaters were being tossed on the floor of the pickup. I made sure everybody had their winter coats because, in Texas, you just never know. High seventies at noon, sleet by three. It happens. Trust me.

Although Willis tends to drive like an eighty-year-old grandpa, we made record time and got to Austin in just over an hour and a half. Graham called me on my cell phone when we were little more than a half-hour out. 'I'll put you on speaker,' I told him.

'Dad's with you?' he asked.

'And us!' Megan shouted out.

'Jesus, Mother! What the hell—'

'Just tell us what's happening,' I interrupted.

'He's dead all right. That's what the EMTs said anyway.'

'How?' Willis asked.

'Stab wounds. Lots of 'em,' Graham said, his voice low. Then he said, 'Mom—'

'What do the police say?' I interrupted yet again. I didn't want his sisters thinking he might have done such a horrible thing. I knew, obviously better than my son, that there was no way in hell he could have done this – awake *or* asleep.

'They just asked me lots of questions. Like when I last talked to him, or saw him, and did I hear anything during the night. Stuff like that.'

'And did you? Hear anything?' Willis asked.

'No. I was asleep,' Graham said.

'Where are you now?' I asked him.

'At that bagel place across the drag,' he said. Graham's dorm was on the south side of campus, close to Guadalupe Street, with McMillan Hall, the dorm Graham had been in since his freshman year, on one side and businesses that catered to the college crowd on the other. That section of Guadalupe Street that bordered the university was universally called the drag.

'We'll be there as quickly as possible,' I told him, said goodbye and rang off.

'You're going to have to drop us off and try to find a parking space,' I told Willis.

'I know, I know,' he said. He'd lived in that same dorm back in the early eighties when the two of us had met. Shortly thereafter we'd moved into a small apartment together, but we both knew that parking anywhere around the university was difficult if not impossible.

We left our bags in the pickup as we'd need to find rooms for all of us since there was no way Graham would be allowed back in his dorm room. The girls and I hopped out of Willis's truck on the drag and headed to the bagel shop. Graham was sitting at a table by the window that overlooked the drag, keeping an eye out, and waved half-heartedly when he saw us.

I'm sure the last person my son wanted to see was Alicia, our foster daughter. The two had become an item a year or so back – an item that thankfully didn't last long. Willis and I thought about forbidding it but knew that would just make the idea all the more attractive. When Graham's old girlfriend came back into town, the relationship between Alicia and Graham had died a natural death. The two had pretty much avoided each other since then. Difficult to do, however, since when Graham was home they lived in the same house. Somehow, they managed it.

Alicia hung back as Megan, Bess and I rushed into the bagel shop and accosted Graham with hugs and questions. He allowed the hugs – just barely – and shrugged at the questions.

Finally he said, 'Y'all know as much as I do.'

'You haven't talked to the police again?' I asked.

'No,' he said.

'Do they know where you are?' I asked.

He shrugged. 'I don't know. Maybe.'

'You didn't tell them where they could find you?' I asked, getting a little anxious.

'They didn't ask,' was his reply.

'So who did it?' Megan asked, wide-eyed.

'How the hell should I know?' Graham demanded a trifle loudly. OK, a lot loudly. The bagel shop was pretty crowded this mid-morning and many heads turned at his outburst.

Backing off, Megan said, 'Jeez, I was just asking! Lighten up!'

'Lighten up?' he said, standing and fisting his hands at his side. 'Lighten up? You lighten the fuck up!'

'Graham, keep it down,' I suggested, touching his shoulder.

He pulled away from my touch. 'I just want to get the hell out of here!' he said, and I could see he was trying hard to hold back his emotions. It wasn't working, but he was trying.

Willis found us about then and went to his son, embracing him. That's all it took. Graham broke down, clinging to his father and sobbing.

I took the girls, all three of them, and moved out to the drag.

I left all four kids with Willis and crossed Guadalupe to Graham's dorm, taking the elevator to the fourth floor, the location of the room shared by my son and the victim – formerly Bishop Alexander. There was a uniformed policeman at the door, barring my way.

'I'm the mother of the roommate of the victim,' I said. 'I need to let whoever's in charge know we're taking Graham to a hotel.'

The uniform nodded and called into the room. 'Detective, roommate's mother's here.'

A man broke away from all the others who were standing around looking down at, I presumed, the body of my son's roommate. When the detective moved toward me it left an opening with a view of the body. I craned my neck to see what I could see – not because I'm one of those people who like to look at car wrecks on the freeway but because I have a knack, you might say, for solving crimes. The detective frowned at me and I straightened up. He probably wouldn't understand.

He was maybe fifty years old, tall and nice-looking, with salt-and-pepper hair and a Magnum, P.I. mustache. He looked like he worked out. There was no tummy hanging over his belt, which had a Texas star as a buckle. He was wearing an actual suit, which, to my untrained eye, looked expensive. Since my husband doesn't own a suit, I have no real experience in that area.

'Mrs Pugh?' he asked, holding out his hand. 'I'm Nate Champion.'

I shook the proffered hand and acknowledged that, yep, that was me. 'I need to take my son somewhere, a motel or hotel. Needless to say, he's very upset.'

'I can imagine,' Detective Champion said.

It dawned on me that I said, '*I* need to take *my* son.' Not, '*My husband and I* need to take *our* son.' Or even, '*We* need to take *our* son.' I wondered why. Well, he *was* quite good-looking. I mentally shook myself.

Getting down to business, I said, 'I'd also like to get him a change of—'

'I can't let you take anything out of the room at this point, ma'am,' the detective said.

I nodded. 'If you have a card, I can call you when we find a place and let you know where we are.'

He pulled a cardholder out of his breast pocket and took out a card. 'That would be great, ma'am,' he said. 'But I'll need your son to come down to the station later today to sign a statement. Do you know where we're located?'

I nodded. 'I went to school here. The station's still downtown, right?'

'Yes, ma'am, on Eighth Street.'

'Right where I left it,' I said and smiled. He didn't smile back. Oh my God, I was flirting. A dead body of a boy on the floor a few feet away and here I was, flirting! Not to mention my husband across the street dealing with our traumatized children. I knew at some point I was going to feel guilty about that. I thanked him for the card and headed back to the elevator.

TWO

Detective Champion had definitely noticed that the victim's roommate's mother was flirting with him. On any other day he would have jumped at the chance to get to know a redhead with the body of, as his father used to say, a brick outhouse. But seeing that there was a good possibility he was going to be arresting her son, he decided now might not be a good time to flirt back.

The kid had seemed very forthcoming when he'd talked to him earlier, even giving him the name of the vic's ex-girlfriend, saying how she keyed his car twice and sent the vic a box of Ex-Lax brownies. Champion had had a girl play that one on him back in college and he almost lost his basketball scholarship because of the days he missed. But, as far as he was concerned, that gave the vic a motive to kill his ex, not the other way around.

He'd just gotten back to his workstation after interviewing the ex-girlfriend, Gretchen Morley, at her ritzy sorority house, and things weren't looking good for the Pugh kid. Champion had had to break the news to the girl and she'd broken down, clinging to him and sobbing like her heart was broken. She *was* just a kid, but he hadn't minded holding on to her. She was as close to beautiful as he'd ever seen. Honey-blonde hair, turquoise-blue eyes, a peaches-and-cream complexion and full, pouty lips. While he'd been holding her, and after his temptation to flirt with the Pugh kid's mother, he'd thought maybe it was time he started dating again. He'd been divorced now for six whole weeks.

Champion had finally got her to sit down in the chair by her desk, taking the chair at the matching desk for himself. If she had a roommate, she hadn't been visible to Champion.

'I'm so sorry for your loss,' he'd said to the girl.

'Thank you,' she'd said, stifling a sob. 'It's just so sudden! A car wreck?'

'No.' He'd cleared his throat. This was the second hardest part of the job. The first hardest was telling someone their loved one was dead – telling them their loved one had been murdered was almost as hard. 'I'm sorry to say he was stabbed to death.'

Gretchen's hands had flown to her mouth as she'd attempted to stifle a small scream. 'Who on earth?'

'We don't know that as yet. Do you know if he had any enemies?' Champion had asked.

'You mean other than his roommate?' she'd countered.

'Graham Pugh was considered an enemy?'

'Well, I mean, outwardly they got along OK, but Bish . . .' She'd sobbed at the mention of his name. 'Bish told me he woke up in the middle of the night more than once and saw Graham sitting up in bed, staring at him. And Bish said, "If looks could kill . . ."' Her hands had flown to her mouth again and she'd sobbed.

'Miss Morley . . .' Champion had started.

'Call me Gretch,' she'd said with a small smile.

'Miss Morley, did you ever see Graham Pugh show any animosity toward Bishop?'

'No, not really. Not me, anyway, but I heard about fights the two had. Last semester everybody was talking about it.'

'Who's everybody?' Champion had asked.

'Well, let's see.' She'd put a pinkie to her lower lip and stared off into space. 'I'm trying to remember where I heard it.'

'Did Bishop tell you about it?'

'No, no, that was before we started dating. I think Lexie Thurgood told me.'

'Lexie Thurgood? Where do I find her? Or him?' Champion had written the name down on his pad.

'Definitely a her. She lives at McMillan Hall, just like Bish does . . .' She'd sobbed. 'I mean did!' She'd put her hands over her entire face this time and rocked as she'd sobbed.

Champion couldn't help thinking this one was going to make some young man's life a living hell. But, he thought, it might just be worth it.

He'd gone to the admin office after he'd left Gretchen Morley's dorm room and checked out Lexie Thurgood. She was a sophomore and did live at McMillan Hall, on the same floor as Bishop and his roommate, just a different wing.

He had been hitting on all cylinders that day, finding Lexie at home just like he'd found Gretchen. It usually didn't work out that well. Lexie had already heard about the death and had actually been in the hall watching 'the action,' as she called it. He thought possibly she was a basketball player. If she wasn't, the Lady Longhorns were missing a bet. She was almost his height, six foot and four inches, wiry but not skinny, with a long face and short hair. She wasn't unattractive. *Yeah*, he'd thought. *I need to start dating again for damn sure.*

After she'd invited him in and he'd sat down – her on her twin bed, he on her desk chair – he'd said, 'Gretchen Morley told me you told her about a big fight Bishop Alexander and Graham Pugh got into last semester.'

She'd shrugged. 'Well, it wasn't that big. They weren't beating each other up or anything. Just yelling at each other. Got kinda heated. Lots of "Fuck you" and "No, fuck you," and crap like that.'

'Where was this?' Champion had asked.

'In the hall. Close to their room, I think. I'd just gotten off the elevator and had to pass by them.'

'Did you stop?' he'd asked.

Lexie had grinned. 'Not where they could see me. Of course, the way they were going at it, I doubt they would have even noticed me. But I sorta stopped close enough where I could hear what was going on.'

'And what *was* going on?' Champion had asked.

Lexie had shrugged. 'Never did find out. Like I said, they were just throwing F-bombs all over the place.'

'No shoving, anything like that?' he'd asked.

Again, she'd shrugged. 'Not that I saw. Of course, I didn't stay for the whole thing. Like I said, just F-bombs. That can get boring after a bit.'

'I can imagine,' he'd said. Standing, he'd added, 'Well, thank you for your time, Miss Thurgood. If you think of anything else, or hear anything else, you'll let us know?'

She'd stood and walked him to the door. 'Definitely,' she'd

said. 'I mean, like I never thought Graham could get violent but, you know, you never know.'

He'd left McMillan Hall thinking he now had two people who thought Graham Pugh was a likely suspect.

We found a motel near IH 35 that didn't cost an arm and a leg and had two double rooms next to each other. We put the girls in one and had Graham share the other with us. I wanted him close. I didn't know if, or probably when, he was going to totally lose it. I thought it best that Willis and I were within reach. They were run-of-the-mill motel rooms, their only outstanding feature the small fridges in each room. Willis took the girls to the nearest grocery store with a small list I'd made of necessities. Orange juice, sodas, bottled water, cookies and chocolate. This was a traumatic situation: chocolate was definitely called for.

When those four were gone, I had a chance to talk to my son.

'Did you tell Dad I did it?' he asked me, sitting on 'his' bed, his arms dangling between his legs, his head bent to face the floor.

'You *didn't* do it,' I said. 'And there was no reason for me to tell your dad that you did.'

'Mom,' he said, finally looking at me. 'What if I did? I mean, God, I really hated the guy! I was even thinking about killing him! And then . . . And then . . . Jeez, Mom, if I didn't do it, what the hell?'

'Did you wake up with blood all over you?' I asked him.

'No,' he said.

'How could you have stabbed him in your sleep and not have blood all over you the next morning? All over you, your bed linens, the floor by your bed!'

'Oh,' he said. 'Yeah.' He perked up. 'Maybe I didn't do it!' he said, looked at me and attempted to smile.

'Honey, there's no way,' I said, reaching across the space between the two queen-sized beds to touch his arm. 'You didn't do it, OK?'

'Maybe,' he said, the smile fading. 'Maybe I didn't. But who the hell did?' he asked, his voice rising. 'And why didn't they kill me too?'

'Maybe because you haven't pissed off as many people as Bishop had?' I suggested.

He nodded. 'Well, that's the God's honest truth. I don't think it would be possible to do that.'

I called Detective Champion after my talk with Graham, to let him know where we were staying, and he suggested, yet again, that I bring Graham to the station to sign his statement. I got his location in the large police building on Eighth Street in downtown Austin and, when Willis and the girls got back, I took Willis's pickup – which I hate to drive, but one does what one must – and Graham and I headed downtown.

I hadn't been in that building since the day I got detained (not arrested, mind you) with fourteen of my closest friends having a sit-in in front of the home-economics department at the university. We were trying to get them to change the name and allow men into the classes. I think that finally happened but it was after my time.

The place had changed. It looked better. Newer than it had. Brighter. I think maybe they'd refurbished the place. We took an elevator to Detective Champion's floor and found his cubicle.

'Mrs Pugh,' he said, extending his hand. We shook. 'Graham,' he said and shook hands with my son. 'Why don't we take this to one of the small conference rooms. More privacy.'

'Sure,' I said and smiled tentatively. He didn't smile back. Jeez, I had to stop this.

But once we got into the 'small conference room,' I knew I wouldn't be smiling much at Champion again. It looked a lot more like an interrogation room to me. Scarred table with graffiti all over it, an obvious two-way mirror and a door that he locked behind him. Why he was allowing me in here I wasn't sure. Maybe he thought Graham was underage, but he was fairly stupid if that was what he thought. Yes, my crush was definitely over.

'Where's my son's statement?' I asked, holding Graham's arm to keep him from sitting down.

'We'll get to that,' Champion said, taking a seat. 'Please, won't you both sit down?'

'I don't think so,' I said, still holding Graham's arm. 'We're here to sign a statement, not be stuck in an obvious interrogation room. We'd like to leave now.'

'Ma'am,' Champion said, his voice getting stern, 'I wanted to give you the benefit of sitting in on this interview, but, seeing as how your son's an adult, I could certainly ask you to leave.'

'Mom, let's just hear him out,' Graham said, pulling away from me and sitting down. I took the seat next to him, trying not to stare at my reflection in the two-way mirror.

'OK,' Champion said, hitting the record button on a tape player on his side of the table. 'This is Detective Nate Champion, January third, four-thirty p.m. With me are Mrs—'

He turned and looked at me. 'First name?'

'Eloise.'

'Mrs Eloise Pugh and her son, Graham Pugh.' Turning to Graham, he said, 'How were you acquainted with the deceased, Bishop Truman Alexander?'

'He was my roommate,' Graham said.

'How long were the two of you acquainted?'

'We met back in August when we both moved into our dorm room at McMillan Hall on Guadalupe.'

'You both attend or attended the University of Texas at Austin, is that correct?'

'Yes, sir.'

'Did the two of you get along?' Champion asked.

'Pretty much,' Graham answered.

'And what exactly do you mean by "pretty much"?' Champion asked.

Graham shrugged, realized the recorder couldn't pick that up and said, 'I mean, I didn't like him but nobody much did.'

'Did the two of you ever fight?'

'You mean like punch each other out? No, not ever.'

'Verbally fight?' Champion asked.

Again, my son shrugged. 'Yeah, sure. Like I said, he was a pain in the ass— I mean neck.'

'Are you aware that there are witnesses to these very heated verbal exchanges?' Champion asked.

'Wait a damn minute!' I said, putting my hand over Graham's mouth to keep him silent. 'Witnesses to what? And who are these witnesses?'

'Mrs Pugh, I can ask you to leave at my discretion,' Champion said.

I took my hand off Graham's mouth. 'Yeah, I guess,' Graham said. 'I mean, we had a fight once out in the hall so I guess somebody coulda heard it.'

'What was the fight about?' Champion asked.

'That time? Jeez, I don't know. Maybe that was the time he accused me of dating some chick he had the hots for. Or maybe it was the time he accused me of taking some food out of the refrigerator that he said was his. Hell, it didn't have his name on it! Or it coulda been the time he said I left a mess in the bathroom! I don't know! He was always on my case about something! And it was usually bullshit!'

'Is that why you would sit up in bed staring at him in the middle of night?' Champion asked.

'Huh?' Graham said.

'The victim told someone that he would wake up in the middle of the night quite often and find you staring at him. The witness reported that the victim said that if looks could kill, he'd have been dead.'

I stood up. 'Either arrest my son right now or we're out of here. No more questions without our attorney present.'

Graham looked at me with fear in his eyes and all I wanted to do was take him in my arms and tell him mommy was going to take care of everything. But something told me this time it wasn't going to be a boo-boo easily fixed.

THREE

'Did you call Tom?' I asked Willis.

'He's out of town, Robin said,' Willis answered. I'd asked him to call our neighbor Tom Kenney, a criminal attorney, but that wasn't working out.

'Did Robin say when he'd be home?' I asked.

'No, but she gave me a number of a guy here in Austin that Tom uses sometimes. Stuart Freeman.' He held out a slip of paper with an Austin area code. 'You want to call him or you want me to?' Willis asked, thrusting the paper at me to let me know in no uncertain terms what his choice was.

'You do it,' I said.

'You know I'm not good at this sort of thing,' my husband whined.

'You're better at it than I am,' I said. 'You know I don't like lawyers.'

'You don't even know this one! Besides, you like Tom!'

'Tom's different. I like him as a neighbor, not as a lawyer,' I countered.

'That's stupid,' Willis said.

'You're stupid,' I shot back. I'm clever that way.

'It's my head in the noose,' Graham said from his bed where we thought he was asleep – the reason we'd mostly been whispering our argument. 'I'll make the damn call.'

He sat up and reached for the slip of paper still in Willis's hand. Willis moved it out of his reach. 'You gonna pay for it?' Willis asked. Graham didn't respond. 'I think an attorney would rather talk to the person paying the bill.'

'Ah ha!' I said, pointing at him. 'That'll be you! I don't get a book check for another couple of weeks so you have to pay.'

'It's a joint account,' he countered.

'Jesus, you two!' Graham said. 'I need a fucking lawyer!'

'Watch your mouth, son!' Willis said.

'Whatever. Just give me a break, OK? I can't take much more!' Graham said.

Willis and I looked at each other. I'm not sure what my husband was feeling, but shame, embarrassment and guilt were warring with each other in my stunted psyche.

'I'll call,' we both said in unison. Then Willis said, 'I've got the number. I'll do it.' With that he took his cell phone and went into the bathroom to make the call.

I looked at my son. 'Sorry,' I said.

'Yeah. Whatever.'

I sat down on his bed next to him. 'This is all bull, honey, and you know it. As soon as the lawyer presents the fact that there was no blood on you or around you this morning to that asshole Champion, maybe they can get down to the real business of finding out who did this.'

Graham looked up at me with his father's beautiful brown eyes and said, 'Can't you look into it? You do it for everybody else – why not me?'

I sighed. 'For one thing, I get a small amount of cooperation from Luna,' I said, mentioning our next-door neighbor and head homicide detective for the Codderville police department, 'which I doubt I'll get from Champion. And also, I know our area, I know who to talk to, all that stuff. Stuff I haven't a clue about here.'

Graham sat up. 'Yeah, but I do! I know lots of people in our dorm, and some of the girls Bishop dated, and guys he screwed over one way or another. I could help!'

And, I thought, maybe he could. If he didn't end up in jail.

'He'll meet us at his office at nine in the morning,' Willis said, coming back in the room.

'How'd he sound?' I asked.

'Like a lawyer! What do you mean, how'd he sound?' My husband was getting testy.

'Did he sound old? Young? Eager? Bored? You know! How did he *sound*?' I persisted.

'Medium,' was Willis's response.

'Willis, don't make me take you in the bathroom!' I said.

'You and what army?' he said.

Our son sighed. 'Is that what you two do for foreplay?'

'That's enough of that, son!' Willis said.

'No, that's enough of you two acting like this is any other day! Not the day I wake up to the bloody corpse of somebody I wanted to kill! Not the day I think I might have actually done—'

'Graham, stop!' I demanded.

Willis looked at me. 'What's he talking about?'

Graham jumped off his bed and began pacing the room. I averted my eyes as he'd gone to bed in only his boxer briefs. I'd stopped thinking I had any claim to his penis when he was about four.

'Nothing,' I said to my husband.

'Mom! Can it! It's not nothing! It's something!' He turned to his dad and said, 'I might have killed him.'

Willis looked at Graham, then looked at me, then looked back at Graham. 'And why, pray tell, do you think you might have killed him?' he asked, with just the right amount of skepticism that made me take his hand in mine. We were obviously united in the fact that our son did not kill his roommate.

'Because I wished him dead!' Graham said, dropping heavily on his bed. 'I even thought about killing him. Tried to work out a plan—'

'Hum,' said Willis. 'Did you?'

I let go of his hand.

'Kill him?' Graham asked.

'No. Work out a plan,' Willis said.

I took back his hand.

'No, not really.'

'Then how did you go about killing him?' Willis asked.

'In my sleep, I think.'

Willis looked at me and I shrugged my shoulders. 'Not a drop of blood on him this morning, or on his bedding, or anywhere but by Bishop,' I said.

'But that detective said that someone told him that Bishop told someone that—'

'Hearsay,' Willis said. 'Not admissible.'

'Maybe not in a court of law,' Graham said, 'but that detective seemed to find it significant.'

Willis sighed. 'Find what?' he finally asked.

'That someone told him that Bishop said he'd wake up in the middle of the night and find me sitting up in bed, staring at him. And he said that if looks could kill—'

'Yeah, yeah. Whatever. Do you remember doing that?' Willis asked.

'No. That's why I think maybe I've been walking in my sleep or something,' Graham said.

'You've never done that in your life!' I said. 'Believe me, I would have noticed.'

'Yeah, but maybe I started because of the stress.'

'What stress?' Willis demanded.

'Jeez, Dad! I'm in college! Didn't you find that stressful?'

Willis didn't answer. Neither did I. I happened to know that Willis spent a great deal of his time in college smoking some really good weed so his stress levels had been mostly non-existent. I thought about recommending that to my son but decided it probably wasn't a good idea.

Since neither of us answered, Graham went on: 'And having Bishop Alexander as a roommate was more than a little stressful! Like a lot! He'd talk non-stop about nothing then demand you repeat what he said so you could prove you were listening! I gave up that shit the second week! But he sure didn't stop talking. And when I did tune in, he was usually talking about some chick he was gonna bang – sorry, Mom, but that's what he said – when he wasn't saying, well, something cruder. Or he was bad-mouthing somebody. Like his supposed best friend, Bobby Dunston. He talked like he hated him, even bad-mouthed him to his face. God, that guy was a jerk.'

'So there's our first suspect,' I said.

'Huh?' my son and husband said, almost in unison.

'Bobby—'

'Dunston,' Graham filled in.

'Bobby Dunston. Bishop's bestie that he abused. Maybe Bobby got tired of it or maybe Bishop went a little too far.'

Graham was shaking his head. 'Nah. Bobby always just laughed, no matter what Bishop said. I think Bobby thought Bishop was joking.'

'Is he stupid?' Willis asked.

Graham shook his head. 'No. Not stupid. Naive, maybe. Actually, he's real smart. On a full ride for scholastic achievement or something.'

'Anyone else you can think of?' I asked.

'Hum, yeah. Maybe. Gaylord Fuchs was Bishop's student adviser. Bishop called him "Gay Fucks" constantly. They were always fighting over his schedule. Bishop always wanted ridiculous classes he couldn't and shouldn't take. I heard through the grapevine he came on to Fuchs' wife once. The story was that Gaylord caught Bishop feeling his wife up without her permission at a student party at their house. Took a punch at him.'

Willis and I looked at each other. 'Now *that's* interesting,' Willis said.

Graham shrugged. 'According to my source, Fuchs' punch went wide and he ended up hitting the wall.' He shrugged again. 'Not that it would have done much damage. Fuchs is about as big as a very skinny ten-year-old.'

'Who would need a weapon to do any real harm,' I said, looking at my husband with a smile on my face.

'Absolutely,' Willis agreed.

'Let's keep going: tell me about Bishop,' I said. 'His personal life.'

Graham shrugged. 'I tried to ignore him and anything to do with him.'

'Surely something got through, if only by osmosis,' Willis said.

'Parents?' I asked.

'Yeah, he had a mom. She came here once to see him. Stayed about fifteen minutes, checking her watch the entire time. She's some big wig at an oil company in Houston. She had a meeting at the Capitol and just stopped by for a minute.'

'That's the only time you ever saw her?' I asked.

'Yeah. She might have come by some other time, but if she did Bishop never mentioned it, and, believe me, Bishop mentioned *everything*!'

'But if you weren't listening?' Willis said.

'Yeah, well, there is that,' Graham conceded.

'What about phone calls to or from his mom?' I asked.

'I heard him call her a couple of times and leave messages on her machine. If she ever called back, I never heard it.'

'What about his father?' Willis asked.

'He never mentioned having one, and I never asked. Far as I know, he was hatched,' Graham said.

'Siblings?' I tried.

Graham shook his head. 'Only child. And, boy, did he act like it! His mom sent him a check every month that was supposed to last him the whole month and he'd blow through it in a couple of days. That's usually what his phone messages to her were about. Send more money.'

'Did she?' I asked.

Graham shrugged. 'Don't know. He tried to borrow money from me a couple of times but I think he finally got the message that I wasn't giving him squat.' He added, 'I saw the check one time – it was for eight hundred dollars! Can you imagine? Eight hundred bucks? I mean, y'all send me a hundred a month and—' He stopped cold. Looked at his shoes, then up at us. 'Never mind,' he said.

'Never mind what?' Willis asked.

'What were we talking about?' Graham asked, his face a mask of innocence.

'We send you a hundred dollars a month. Is that not enough?' I asked.

'Ah, well, I could always use more—'

Willis was grinning. 'I know what he was going to say,' my husband said, looking at me. 'Hand me your wallet,' he said to our son.

'Ah, I'm not sure I have it—' Graham started.

'It's on the nightstand,' I said, pointing.

Willis stood and picked up the wallet.

'Hey! I'm over eighteen, you know! You have no right—'

Willis pulled two twenties out of the bill section of Graham's wallet. 'When are you sending him his next check?'

'I mailed it yesterday. He wouldn't have gotten it yet,' I answered, looking at my son.

'So the end to that sentence is we send you a hundred a month and you usually have some left over,' Willis said, staring level at Graham.

'So I'm frugal. Sue me.'

'Maybe we'll just lower the amount—'

'Willis, now is not the time. Besides, I'm proud of him. He's saving money. I find that quite responsible. Certainly not the act of someone who'd kill his roommate.'

Boy, did that bring us all back to reality with a bang.

I sighed. 'We have to be at the lawyer's office by nine a.m.,' I said, looking at the travel clock on the nightstand that showed it was getting close to eleven o'clock. 'We all need to get some sleep.'

Stuart Freeman, the lawyer recommended by our neighbor, had his office in a converted Victorian near downtown. It was a beautiful old place, with original hardwood floors, crown moldings and tin ceilings. I came down with a bad case of house envy the minute we stepped in. A young, very pregnant woman stood up from a desk in the entry hall and came toward us, all smiles, both hands holding her belly. I was familiar with the gesture.

'When are you due?' I asked.

'Last week,' she said and grinned. 'You're the Pughs?' she asked.

Willis nodded.

'I'm Maggie. Stuart will be with you in a minute. He's on a call. Won't y'all have a seat?'

The entry hall was furnished with four mismatched comfy chairs that made the house even more desirable. We only had to wait a few minutes before a large pocket door opened and a man walked out, his hand held out to Willis. Like Champion, he was in his fifties, with a full head of wavy white hair but tanned skin and blue eyes and a cleft in his chin. I started wondering if maybe Willis and I weren't having sex often enough. I was certainly finding other men attractive all of a sudden.

'Mr Pugh, I just got off the phone with Tom Kenney,' he said, mentioning our neighbor, the lawyer whose wife had referred us to Stuart Freeman. 'He said to send you his regards and to tell you that if he can do anything to help, just call him.'

'I appreciate that, Mr Freeman,' Willis said, shaking his hand.

'Stuart, please,' he said, turning to me to shake my hand.

'E.J.,' I said. 'And he's Willis.'

Turning to our son, he said, 'You must be Graham.'

'Yes, sir,' he said, shaking the proffered hand.

'Why don't we go in my office and talk about this mess,' Freeman said.

'Yes, sir,' Graham said and followed the lawyer into his private office.

My house envy would have been through the roof if I hadn't been so worried about Graham. The same hardwood floors, the same crown molding, the same tin ceiling, but part of the hardwoods were covered with an antique oriental rug – I could tell it was antique by the fact that it was well-worn – and leather visitors' chairs that also looked well-worn and well-loved. There was the biggest slab of mahogany I'd ever seen, with a patina to die for topping off a beautiful, mostly bare desk. There was a fireplace with a marble surround and a thick oak mantle. The walls were a muted green and covered with degrees, citations and pictures of Stuart Freeman with a lot of people I recognized from high local, state and even federal government positions. I could only hope this meant we'd come to the right place.

'Please, have a seat,' Freeman said as he sank into a much larger, antique leather chair. 'Can I have Maggie get you anything? Coffee, tea?'

'No, we're fine,' I said before Willis could suggest a cup of coffee from the overly pregnant young woman. I didn't want her going into labor because Willis thought he needed caffeine.

'OK, then, let's get down to business,' Freeman said, leaning his elbows on his desktop and clasping his hands together. 'All I know at this moment is that there was a death. Want to fill me in?'

So we did, each taking a turn, with me emphasizing the fact that Graham had not been covered with blood when he awoke the day before.

'That's a good point, E.J.,' Freeman said. 'We need to make

that fact abundantly clear to the detective. Do we have proof of that?'

We three Pughs looked at each other. I had no idea. What would prove that Graham had no blood on him?

'What were you wearing to bed?' I asked my son.

'Boxer briefs,' he said.

'The same ones you wore last night?' I asked.

'Jeez, Mom! I do know to change underwear occasionally!'

'So where are the briefs you were wearing?' I asked.

'In the hamper in the bathroom,' he answered.

'Unfortunately, the police can assume you got rid of any bloody clothing,' Freeman said.

'Luminol!' I shouted. Sort of like 'Eureka!'

Freeman looked at me and sat back in his chair. 'Good thinking, E.J. We'll insist that the police luminol the entire dorm room.' He looked at Graham. 'Will they find anything if they do that?'

'That's the stuff that shows blood even after it's been cleaned up, right?' Graham asked.

'Right,' Freeman answered.

Graham shrugged. 'I don't see why they would. I haven't cut myself or anything. And, Mr Freeman, I didn't—'

'Don't tell me, son. I'm not asking if you did it and I don't want you to tell me if you did or didn't. We're just going to prove that you couldn't have. That OK with y'all?' he asked.

I wanted to shout, 'Of course he didn't do it, you asshole!' but I kept my mouth shut. He was going to *prove* that Graham hadn't done it. That was enough for me.

FOUR

We left Freeman's office and headed back to the motel, where the girls were waiting for us in the restaurant adjacent to the motel, having partaken of a particularly expensive breakfast, the remnants of which lay spread out before them.

'Full enough?' I asked, raising an eyebrow.

Megan burped in response then giggled. Bess said, 'I was very hungry,' while Alicia piped in with, 'I only had toast. And coffee. And some fruit.' She looked at both her sisters, who were looking back at her with evil eyes. 'Well, I did! Y'all are the ones who ate everything in sight!'

'Did not!' Bess said, while Megan just burped again.

'Y'all are going to have to go home,' I said. Everyone turned to stare at me. 'Not because of breakfast, for crying out loud. Because you can't miss any more school and your dad can't miss any more work. Your dad doesn't work, we don't get money. No money, no lawyer for your brother. And you three, no school, no graduation. You want to repeat your senior year?'

Megan fell back in her chair, crossing her arms over her chest and said, 'Whatever!'

Bess said, 'You have a point, Mom,' while Alicia merely looked anywhere but at Graham.

'She's right,' Willis said, sitting down at the table. Graham and I followed suit. I noticed he grabbed the chair furthest from Alicia, meaning I was sitting next to my foster daughter. I patted her on the leg and she gave me a weak smile. I knew this wasn't easy for her. I thought she might still be in love with my son. He'd been the one to call it off, having decided to get back with his ex-girlfriend. That reconciliation hadn't lasted long and I had to wonder if it hadn't been an excuse to stop his relationship with Alicia. It had been an uncomfortable situation, our foster daughter and our birth son falling in love, and, sensing that, Graham might have actually acted like

an adult – sort of – and figured out a way to stop it. Maybe
not the best way but it had worked. I decided I needed to find
something to take Alicia's mind off Graham, and what could
be better than another boy? Sexist, you say? Absolutely not.
You fall off a horse, you get back on a horse. A boy breaks
your heart, you find one who won't. And still get your Ph.D.
And become CEO.

We'd left Stuart Freeman's office with the knowledge that
he'd call Detective Champion and let him know he was representing Graham, and suggest – strongly, I hoped – that they
luminol the entire dorm room. It was Tuesday already and the
girls had lost one and a half days of school, while Willis had
two projects he was supposed to be winding up and a couple
of would-be clients he needed to schmooze. On their way
home, they dropped Graham and me off in his dorm building
parking lot so we could get his car – a rather beat-up late-
nineties Toyota Celica that had no air conditioning, heater,
radio or much of a paint job. I couldn't help thinking nostalgic-
ally about my two-seater Audi sitting at home in the garage.
That would have been perfect for taking on the hills of Austin.

I called Stuart Freeman's very pregnant assistant, told her
Willis was leaving town and gave her my cell number for
Stuart to call if and when something came up. She assured
me she would. She was breathing rather heavily and I figured
the baby was probably dancing on her lungs (Megan was big
on that in vitro). I had a feeling Stuart was going to be fielding
his own calls in a matter of days, if not hours.

Graham and I went back to the motel. I didn't bother cance-
ling the room the girls had been in. Graham could move in
there – we both probably needed a little space. I knew I did,
and I could only imagine how much my son needed it. Once
alone in my motel room, I called Elena Luna, my next-door
neighbor and the head homicide detective for the Codderville
police department. Although we both lived in another jurisdiction – Black Cat Ridge, which has its own police force – she
and I had worked several cases together. OK, maybe half a
dozen or more. She grudgingly, but since I had a tendency to
trip over dead bodies (as my family put it; my take is that I
just happened to often be in the wrong place at the right – or

wrong – time), we have worked side by side, often to her horror. But, still, we were friends. She was probably my best friend now, after the death of Bess's birth mother when Bess was only four. It had taken a while to think that role of BFF could ever be filled, but in a lot of ways it has been – by Luna. Just, please, don't tell her.

I called her at the police station in Codderville. I have her direct line, one she's tried to get changed often but the brass won't let her do it. So I still call it whenever I'm in the mood.

'Luna,' she said upon answering.

'It's me.'

'Joy.'

'You don't know what's happened,' I said.

'And now you're going to tell me,' she said.

'Graham's roommate was murdered last night and Graham's the prime suspect.'

There was a moment of silence on the other end of the line. I tried one of her own tactics on her: I kept quiet and let the silence mount.

Finally, she said, 'Is this a joke?'

'That would be a pretty sick joke,' I said.

'But not beyond you,' she said.

'No, it's not a joke. I'm in Austin. Willis and the girls were here with us but they're on their way back. I'm staying here with Graham.'

'Who's handling the case?'

'Austin,' I said, like *duh*.

'I mean who? On the homicide detail?'

'A Detective Champion,' I answered.

'Nate Champion? Fifties, looker?'

'That's him,' I said and tried to contain the sigh I knew was just inches away from my mouth.

'He's good,' Luna said. 'I worked with him on a task force back in the day. Smart. Mention my name.'

'And maybe he won't arrest my son?' I asked.

'I wouldn't go that far. If there's evidence, Graham will be arrested, Pugh, you know that. Is there evidence?'

So I explained about the stabbing and the blood and the fact that Graham had none on him.

'And you saw him immediately after he discovered the body?'

'No, of course not! It took maybe an hour and a half to gather the troops and get here to Austin.'

'So you don't really know if there was blood on Graham or not?'

I took the phone away from my ear and looked at it. Finally, I put it back and said, 'Who the hell's side are you on, Luna?' OK, maybe I didn't say it – maybe I screamed it.

'Whoa, Mama. I'm looking at this from Nate's point of view. I know Graham, he doesn't. But if you mention me he might be more polite.'

'I don't give a rat's ass about polite, Luna! I want them to find out who really did this and stay away from my son!'

'Of course you do,' she said, her voice soft. Again, I took the phone away from my ear. Luna never talks to me in a soft voice. Ever. This wasn't going well.

'Don't patronize me, Luna!'

'I'm not. Look, I have a few days' vacation built up. Want me to come down there?'

'I have a double room,' I said.

'Let me talk to Eduardo' – Luna's husband – 'and I'll get back to you. But save that bed.'

'Luna?'

'Yeah?'

'Ah. Thanks?'

'Whatever,' she said, and hung up.

Nate Champion decided he'd go with the crime-scene techs when they luminoled the vic's dorm room. Stuart Freeman had called him, told him he was representing Graham Pugh and suggested that they luminol the Pugh kid's bed, clothes, the floor around him, *ad nauseum*. Champion figured it couldn't hurt but he was only hours away from finding the kid, Mirandizing him and bringing him in, the well-stacked mother be damned. She was just going to have to face it: her kid was a murderer. Of course, he knew Stuart Freeman personally and by reputation. He was a nice guy – if you liked pit bulls. So Champion knew he'd have to have all his ducks in a row on this one.

He stood by the closed door of the dorm room, close to the light switch, while the techs hung a blackout curtain on the one window and sprayed the entire room with luminol. Champion wasn't the scientific sort and had no idea what was in the stuff. All he knew was once you sprayed it, turned out the lights and hit the stuff with a black light, blood showed up really well.

'The lights, Detective,' one of the crime-scene techs said and Champion hit the switch, bringing the room pretty close to darkness. Using the black light, the tech started walking the room. The blood around the vic's bed, on the floor, and even some on the ceiling, showed up great. But that was about it. The rest of the room was clear.

That is, until the tech stripped Graham Pugh's bed and sprayed the mattress. Then the black light showed a large patch of blood.

'Interesting,' Champion said.

'Lights,' the tech said and Champion again flipped the switch. 'What?' the tech asked. 'You think the kid did it, then got rid of his clothes and sheets and shit?'

'Could be,' Champion said, staring at the spot on the mattress that had shown blood stains under the black light. 'Yeah, could be.'

My cell phone rang as Graham and I were coming back from dinner. I saw it was Stuart Freeman and answered, saying, 'Let us get in the room, Stuart. Just a second.' The temp had dropped drastically with the sunset and I wanted to get inside before hypothermia set in.

We hurried into my room and I put the phone on speaker. 'Graham's with me. What's up?'

'We've got a problem,' he said without preamble. 'They did the luminol testing.'

'And?' I asked, puzzled. Surely that would clear Graham.

'There was blood on Graham's mattress,' Stuart said.

I looked at my son, who was looking back at me. Then I saw something in his eyes and his face turned red. 'Graham?' I said.

'Ah,' he started. Then got up and left the room.

'Graham!' I called after him.

'E.J.? What's going on?' Stuart asked.

'I don't know! He just got up and walked out. Stuart, let me call you back!' I said and hung up the phone, the door knob already in my hand as I headed to my son's room next door.

I knocked but got no answer. 'Graham, open this door! If you don't, I'll call the desk and tell them I think you're in trouble and have them unlock it! Do you want me to do that?'

The door opened. All I got was my son's back as he headed to one of the queen-sized beds and sat down, his head in his hands.

I came in and shut the door behind me. 'What's going on?'

'I can't,' he mumbled.

'You can't what?' I asked, sitting down next to him.

'Nothing,' he mumbled.

I pulled his hands away from his face. 'Graham! Damn it! What's going on?'

'I can't tell you,' he said, his head down.

'Why the hell not?' I demanded.

Finally, he looked at me. 'Because you're my mom.'

That took me aback. I sat there looking at him, then said, 'Can you tell your dad?'

He was quiet for a moment, then sighed and said, 'Yeah, I guess I have to.'

My cell phone was still in my hand, so I hit the number that would instantly call Willis's. He answered on speaker phone.

'Hey, babe! Everything OK?' he asked.

'Maybe not. Are you home yet?'

'No, just passing through Codderville. Should be home in a few minutes. What's going on?'

'Call Graham on his cell phone as soon as you get there,' I said. 'And not on speaker. And not around the girls. Take it in our bedroom, OK?'

'Ah, yeah, OK. What the fuck—'

I hung up and looked at my son. 'Will that work?'

He sighed again. 'It'll have to,' he said.

I left his room and went to mine, immediately calling Willis's number again. 'Take me off speaker,' I said when he answered.

'What?' he said.

'Did you pull over?'

'No—'

'We don't talk on our cell phones while driving, unless we're on speaker, Willis. What kind of example are you setting—'

'Yeah, right, whatever. I'm pulling over.'

'Then step out of the car,' I said.

'What the shit is going on?' he demanded.

'Are you pulled over yet?'

'I'm taking an exit now. Just hold on, I'm putting the phone down. You know, bad example—'

'Shut up,' I said, not sure that he had heard me since there was no answer. I could hear the engine noise of his truck and the girls talking – mostly asking their father what was going on.

Finally, I heard a door slam and Willis say, 'OK, now what?' So I told him.

'Blood on his mattress? And he'll only talk to me?'

'That's about it,' I said.

Then he said, 'Oh!'

'Oh, what?' I demanded.

'Nothing,' he said, 'I've gotta get home so I can call him.'

'Then you call me immediately and tell me what's going on.'

'Um, well—'

'Willis!'

'Probably,' he said and hung up.

I sat in my motel room with the phone in my hands for what seemed like hours. And maybe it was. Finally, it rang and I saw Willis's name on the screen. 'What?' I demanded.

'OK, honey, here's the thing . . .' Willis started.

'What?' I yelled, then caught myself. Graham could probably here that in the next room, so I whispered, 'What?'

'He busted a cherry,' my husband said.

'What?' I asked again, wondering if that was the only word I knew, then it dawned on me. 'Oh my God,' I said. 'Whose?'

'He didn't go into detail. He said he didn't know she was a virgin and he felt really bad about it, and he was only with her that one time—'

'One time? You take a girl's virginity, you don't instantly drop her—' I started, on a roll.

'Now's not the time, babe. He said he didn't even know her name. They met at a party and they were both drunk—'

'Oh my God! Did you teach him nothing? You're his father, for God's sake! You have a responsibility—'

'Now's not the time! The problem is he doesn't know her name. So we might have a problem proving it isn't Bishop's blood.'

That stopped me cold. Then I said, 'What about DNA and all that stuff? Wouldn't that prove it?'

'I don't know, honey. Depends on how well our son cleaned up the mess.'

'Well, shit!' I said. 'At least I taught him how to clean. Now we're in real trouble!'

FIVE

'Hey, Nate,' Carl Rios said, leaning on the wall of Nate Champion's cubical.

'Hey, Carl, what's up?'

Carl Rios was the senior crime-scene tech and took care of all the evidence brought in from the scene. 'Gonna piss you off,' he said.

Detective Champion frowned. 'Just tell me.'

'That blood on the roommate's mattress?'

'Yeah?'

'Pretty damn old. And definitely not the vic's. If I could venture an educated guess, I'd say the roommate had female company, and either she was on the rag or new to the big it,' Rios said.

'Damn,' Champion said. Then, looking up at Rios, said, 'Don't tell the kid's lawyer. Not yet.'

'Hey, man, I don't talk to lawyers! Ever. Last one I talked to managed to get everything I own to give to my ex! 'Sides, talking to lawyers is not part of my job description.'

'Yeah, whatever. Shit!'

'You really liked the kid for it, huh?'

'What's not to like? He'd sit up in the middle of the night and stare at the vic like he wanted to kill him,' Champion said.

'Who told you that?' Rios asked.

Champion thought about it. 'Never mind. Thanks,' he said, got up from his desk, got his service revolver out of the drawer where he kept it and headed out the door, thinking, *Yeah, who told you that, stupid?*

I was in a quandary: did I talk to my son about what Willis had just told me? Did I chastise him for getting drunk? Ask him if he was too drunk to use a condom? Give him hell for not getting the girl's name and trying to make amends of some sort? Of course, how does one make amends for that? Dinner and a movie didn't seem like a good choice. Was he sure she gave consent? Oh my God. Did Graham take real advantage of this drunken coed? Was there some poor girl out there thinking she'd been raped but not knowing who her abuser was? My stomach was in knots and I felt like vomiting. All those talks we'd had, my son and I, throughout high school, about respecting girls. About thinking of someone doing that to one of his sisters. About respect. About all that stuff you try to teach a boy. Did all that fly out the window when he had too many beers in him? Is that what happened?

I tried to calm myself down. I didn't know what had happened with this unnamed girl. But I needed to find out, and I needed to keep calm while trying to find out. I took a few deep breaths and left my room, went to Graham's and knocked on the door.

And all the effort of trying to calm down disappeared. 'Did you rape that girl?' I demanded on seeing my son.

His eyes got huge as he backed away from me. 'God, Mom!'

'Did you?' I demanded.

'No! Jesus! What's your deal? Why would you think that?'

I collapsed on the unused queen-sized bed. 'I'm sorry,' I finally managed to get out.

'Jesus! The police are accusing me of murder and now you're accusing me of rape? Fuck!'

'Watch your language and sit down,' I said, without much authority. I was pretty sure I'd blown that. He sat down on the other bed. 'Tell me about it,' I said.

'No! It's none of your business! I can't believe Dad called you and told you! I mean, shit! I can't trust either of you!' At that, he jumped up and fled the room. I was right behind him but not quick enough to stop him from getting in the Celica and taking off, leaving rubber behind him.

'Luna, it's me,' I said into the phone.

'I figured it was you when your name came up on the screen. I'm smart like that.'

'You're a smartass, that's for sure. Look, you need to call that Champion asshole.'

'Pugh—'

'Don't start with me! They found blood on Graham's dorm room mattress—'

'Damn, Pugh—'

'He, well, he had a date.'

'Uh-huh. And?'

'They were drunk and she was a virgin,' I said quickly.

'OK, so it's not the roommate's blood?'

'Of course not! You need to tell Champion that!' I declared.

'He'll figure it out on his own,' she said.

'I don't have time for that shit! Also, when you're talking to him, you need to find out the name of the witness, maybe two witnesses—'

'To what? Somebody saw him do it?'

'Of course not! Bishop told somebody that Graham stared at him at night when he should have been sleeping, and somebody else said they witnessed a fight – a verbal fight – between Graham and Bishop.'

'Bishop's the vic?'

I sighed heavily. 'Of course! Haven't you been listening?'

'Pugh, I'm about to hang up here!'

'No, no, no, don't do that.' I sighed again. 'Elena, I'm terrified. What would you feel if this was one of your boys?'

There was silence for a moment, then she said, 'Terrified. I talked to Eduardo and I'll be heading to Austin tomorrow. You still have that bed for me?'

'Yes. Thank you. Yes!'

'How's Graham holding up?'

'Ah, well, probably not so good.'

Again I heard only silence. Then she said, 'What *aren't* you telling me?'

I could feel sweat – or maybe it was tears – coursing down my face. 'I accused him of raping that virgin.'

'Did he?' she asked.

'Of course not!' I said. Then added: 'I don't think so. I hope not.'

'So he's not speaking to you?' she asked.

'He ran off in his car. I have no idea where he is. Don't tell Champion!'

'I won't. But find him.'

'I don't have wheels! He took the only car we have here.'

'Have you called him?'

'No, I called you instead.'

'Very thoughtful of you,' she said, I think sarcastically. 'Call your son.'

'When are you coming here?' I asked – OK, pleaded.

'OK, I'm leaving now. Just as soon as I hang up the phone from talking to Nate Champion,' she said and hung up on me. I sighed with relief.

Graham hit the drag, going up one side of Guadalupe and down the other. Not doing what one usually does on the drag: looking for friends, cute girls, someone selling weed or tacos or both. There was way too much on Graham's mind to worry about what was happening on the drag. He was trying to remember what the girl looked like. Medium was all his mind could conjure up: medium height, medium-length medium brown hair, medium pretty, medium hot. She was taller than his sister Bess but shorter than his sister Megan. He didn't even contemplate comparing her to Alicia. He wasn't going there. Not now, not ever.

She had to have a name, but did he know it? Where did he meet her? It was at a party, he knew that. Whose? Wait. Dave what's-his-name – that guy – the one who— Wisher! Dave Wisher! On Lamar, near campus. It was coming back to him!

He left the drag and headed for Lamar Blvd. He wasn't drunk when he originally found the place, only when he left. Surely he could remember landmarks. And then there it was: the fourplex where Dave lived, where Dave threw that party. The party where he'd met the girl. The girl who . . . He wasn't going there either. The fourplex faced a side street off Lamar. He turned onto the side street then directly into the small parking lot of the fourplex. It was coming back to him now. It was upstairs, in the back.

He jumped out of the Celica, not even bothering to lock it, and headed up the stairs, two steps at a time. When he found the right door, he just stood there for a moment, breathing heavily. It wasn't from the stairs – he played intramural basketball and was damn good, and fast. No, it was from fear. Something he'd been feeling for two days now: deep down dread. Behind that door would be an answer to one of his questions about his own character: did he molest that girl? Was he a drunken rapist? The answer to that might lead him to answer the other question: was he a murderer?

Taking a deep breath, Graham knocked on the door. He heard a noise inside, someone moving around, then a voice said, 'Just a minute! Hold on!'

The door opened and he saw Dave Wisher standing there, rocking back and forth. Dave always reminded Graham of Shaggy in the 'Scooby-Doo' cartoons. He was tall and thin, with scruffy, sandy-colored hair hanging in his face most of the time, and, most importantly, he was usually stoned.

'Shit, Pugh! Why didn't you say it was you, man? I've been dashing around hiding my stash!' Then he laughed. 'Ha! I dashed my stash!' And he laughed again.

'Dave, you straight enough to answer some questions?' Graham asked.

Dave shrugged. 'Well, man, you know, it *is* like, you know, after five somewhere!' And he laughed again. 'That's what my dad always said when he wanted to get drunk! It's after five somewhere!'

'Dave, I gotta come in. I gotta ask you some questions.'

'Sure, man!' Dave said, opening the door wide and stumbling back. *'Mi casa es su casa!'*

Graham moved inside the sparse one-bedroom apartment. There was a futon for a sofa and beanbags for chairs. TV trays had had their legs sawed down to fit the floor motif. Graham landed on the futon while Dave took a beanbag chair. His first attempt failed and he landed on the floor, laughing, before he picked himself up and nestled his butt into the beanbag.

'You OK?' Graham asked.

'Oh, yeah, man, I'm fine. Just fine. So what's up? You want a joint?'

'No, thanks, not right now. I gotta ask you about that party you had a couple of weeks ago.'

'Which one?'

'The one I came to?'

'Shit, man, I have lots of parties. Don't know who comes to which one, you know?' Dave said.

Graham sighed. Maybe this wasn't going to work, he thought. 'Look, I met a girl here and she came back to my dorm room with me but I didn't get her name—'

'Hey, man, are you the one that broke my cousin's cherry?'

'Ah—'

Dave leaned forward and slapped Graham on the knee, almost falling over when he did so. 'Shit, man, she's been looking for you! Didn't know your name, you know? She thought you were hot! But she couldn't remember where you lived or nothing. Just McMillan. And, man, that's like saying you live in Texas, you know?'

She thought he was hot, which must mean he didn't force her into anything. He wasn't a rapist. Maybe. 'What's her name? Your cousin's?'

'Miranda! With an "m."'

'She got a last name?' Graham asked.

'Sure, man. Just like me. Wisher. Miranda Wisher! You know, if she wasn't my cousin, I'd do her,' Dave said, settling his head back against the beanbag chair.

'Where can I find her?' Graham asked.

'At her place,' Dave said.

'Where's her place, man? Where can I find Miranda?'

'Um, she's like over at the B and B dorm. He parents have big bucks. Her dad and my dad, like they're brothers, ya know? And her dad, like, he invented something – shit, I can't remember what. But he like made millions! My dad, he's a mailman.' Dave shrugged. 'You know the place? The B and B?'

'Yeah, I know it,' Graham said.

'She's over there, man. If she's, like, home, you know?' Dave's eyes were closed now and his words were little more than mumbles, but Graham had what he needed. He made sure the apartment door locked behind him when he left.

Detective Nate Champion knocked on the door of Gretchen Morley's dorm room and waited. And waited. He knocked again. Still no answer. He was turning to leave when his cell phone rang.

'Champion,' he said into it.

'Nate, hey, it's Elena Luna, Codderville P.D. We worked together on that task force back in—'

'Elena, sure! Hi, nice to hear from you. What's up? You in Austin?'

'On my way,' she said. 'The thing is, it's about one of your cases.'

'Yeah? Which one?'

He could hear Elena rustling papers, then she said, 'Bishop Alexander.'

'Yeah, that's my case,' he said, frowning. 'How are you involved?'

'Well, his roommate, Graham Pugh, is the son of a friend of mine. Actually, the Pughs are my next-door neighbors. Good people,' she added.

'Uh-huh,' Champion said. 'And she called you because?'

'Because she's scared, Nate. Wouldn't you be? You've got a boy yourself.'

'My son didn't kill his roommate.'

'And neither did Graham. Nate, I know this boy. I've known him since he was seven years old. He's a good kid. A real good kid.'

'Elena, what did you expect your call to accomplish here? Huh? You think I'm going to put aside this line of questioning because you say the Pugh kid is a good boy? Uh-uh. Doesn't work that way.'

'I know that. Believe me, I know that. But I just want you to keep an open mind. Maybe Graham's not the only one who might be a suspect, you know?'

'I'm a better cop than that, Luna,' he said, obviously not happy with her assumptions. 'Look, check in with me when you get to town but don't go thinking you're gonna be working this case. 'Cause you're not. Got it?'

'Got it,' Luna said.

'How's Eduardo?'

'Home now for almost two years and doing great. How's Margaret?'

'You'd have to ask her new boyfriend,' Champion said.

'Oops. Sorry about that. Divorce sucks.'

'Yeah, I've noticed. Call me when you get in.'

'Right. Bye.'

Champion hung up his cell phone and frowned. He needed to head over to McMillan Hall, the dorm shared by the vic and the Pugh kid. He wanted to check out that room again. Just to be on the safe side.

I knew Graham had missed two days of classes, something he couldn't afford to do. Maybe he should skip this semester? If things kept going the way it was now looking, he might have to. I looked down at my hands and saw they were clenching and unclenching. I didn't realize that until I saw them. I stretched out my fingers to try to relax. It didn't work.

There was a knock on the door and I rushed to it, hoping my son had returned. Instead I found Luna standing there, duffle bag in her hand.

'Oh,' I said. I'm afraid my disappointment showed.

'Happy to see you, too, Pugh,' she said, shoving past me into the motel room.

'Sorry, I thought – hoped – you were Graham.'

'He's still not back?' she asked.

'No,' I said. No need to dwell further on that subject. 'Did you talk to Champion?'

'Yeah,' she said and shook her head. 'Not great. Not horrible but not great. He's keeping an open mind but he still likes Graham for this. You two come up with any leads?'

'Yes!' I said, and rushed to the small table by the window of the motel room where my notepad was. 'Bishop's ex-girlfriend, Gretchen Morley, and his supposed BFF, Bobby Dunston. Seems Bishop dumped Gretchen and she retaliated by keying his car and baking him Ex-Lax brownies. And the BFF, Bobby Dunston – Bishop was big on putting him down constantly and calling him names, in front of other people.'

'So why didn't this Bobby guy just call him out and find a new BFF?' she asked.

I shrugged. 'I have no idea. But there's somebody else, too. Gaylord Fuchs. He was Bishop's student adviser. Bishop came on to his wife and Fuchs caught him, tried to hit him but missed.'

'So maybe he tried again, but this time with a knife?' she suggested.

'My thoughts exactly.'

'Have you told Champion about this guy?' she asked.

I shook my head. 'We're not exactly on speaking terms,' I said.

Luna dumped her duffel bag on one of the beds and sank down. I sat on my own and said, 'Graham didn't do this.'

'I know,' she said. 'But that knowledge doesn't mean shit.'

'Luna—' I started, panic beginning to set in.

She kicked me lightly in the shin. 'We'll take care of it, Pugh. We always do.'

And I thought, *From her lips to God's ears.*

Graham drove to the B&B dorm off Guadalupe. Its actual name was the Baker & Boyle House for Women, but it had been called the B&B since almost its inception in the late sixties. Misters Baker and Boyle were two well-healed attorneys from Dallas who both had daughters graduating high school and entering their freshman year at U.T. Neither Baker nor Boyle thought any of the dorms near the U.T. campus were suitable for their daughters, as some were reportedly going coed, and neither wanted their girls joining a sorority where they might have more freedom than either man would wish. So the B&B was built on a parcel of land near U.T., within chauffeur distance of the campus. It was a large red brick building, rather imposing in a 'we're rich and you're not' sort of way. Graham knew they had maid service and a cafeteria with an actual chef. He wondered if he could just walk in or if he had to have an invitation. Only one way to find out, he figured.

He parked the Celica and got out, locking it this time. He headed up the long walkway to the front doors of the dorm. The chandelier in the foyer was bigger than his Celica and the well-cared-for leather sofas in the living room made the place look more like a high-end men's club than a women's dorm. But there were enough knick-knacks and colorful throw pillows to bring in that feminine touch. The floors were hardwood parquet and the place appeared to have been fairly newly painted. There were girls – or young women, he amended to himself – sitting in the living room chatting; some in the library nook he could see to the left of the entrance, full of leather chairs and books, and some sitting at cafe tables in a dining area, drinking Starbucks coffee from the barista at a small stall in the dining room. A real-life Starbucks stall.

Graham went up to the nearest young woman and asked, 'Could you tell me which room Miranda Wisher is in?'

She looked him up and down and said, 'Lucky Miranda. Third floor, B, elevators over there.' She pointed him in the right direction and he took off.

He took the elevator to Miranda Wisher's floor, found the room and knocked on the door. He knew all of the rooms were singles and so knew Miranda didn't have a roommate. The door opened and a girl was standing there. A girl he instantly recognized, and the entire evening came flooding back. She definitely wasn't medium anything. Lots of curly brown hair cascading down her back, eyes big and brown with black lashes and a body—

'Hi,' he said, trying to stay on track.

'Oh my God!' Miranda yelled and threw her arms around him. 'I've been looking all over for you!'

She took his hand and pulled him into her room. He'd heard the girls who lived at the B&B had to furnish their own rooms and, if so, the room he walked into told him a lot more about Miranda Wisher. To say it was eclectic was an understatement. Dead rock stars adorned the walls, everyone from Kurt Cobain to Buddy Holly, with Jerry Garcia and the 'dead at 27's': Jimi Hendrix, Janis Joplin and Jim Morrison. The wall space left was taken up with half of a carousel pink elephant, its trunk pointed to the ceiling. The antique iron bed was covered with an Indian-print throw and the bedside table was an antique sewing table. A large armchair and ottoman took up one corner – a very sedate armchair and ottoman – covered with a very old tapestry of knights and princesses and castles with turrets. An ornately carved desk against one wall was crowded with books that obviously couldn't fit in the glass-covered barrister cabinets on either side of the desk.

'I finally figured out where we met,' Graham said, omitting as much as possible. 'Dave told me where to find you.'

'He couldn't tell by my description of you who you were. But if you know Dave, you know he's generally stoned out of his head,' she said with a grin.

'Yeah, he's the poster boy for not legalizing weed,' Graham said, returning the grin.

'God, I was so drunk that night! I usually don't drink—' she started, but Graham interrupted.

'I'm sorry. That should never have happened. I was too drunk to realize how drunk you were. If you'd just said, you know, about, well, you know—'

'About being a virgin?' She shrugged then grinned at him again. 'Don't be sorry. I'm not. I'd been looking for the right guy to lose it to. You won.'

Under any other circumstances, Graham might have laughed at that, but instead he said, with not much sincerity, 'Lucky me.'

Miranda cocked her head. 'Something's wrong,' she said. Not a question: a statement.

'Miranda, I'm sorry to dump this on you, but yeah, something's wrong.'

She took his hand. 'Tell me.'

'Did you hear about the murder at McMillan?' he asked.

She nodded.

'That was my roommate, Bishop Alexander. The police think I did it.'

To her credit, she didn't let go of his hand. Graham was thankful for that. 'Why do they think that?' she asked.

'For one thing, the blood on my mattress.'

This time she let go of his hand. 'Oh. That's why you're here. Why you finally started looking for me.'

She stood up and went to the door, opening it. 'You can give the police my name and address. I'll be happy to tell them the blood was mine.'

'Miranda—' Graham started.

'It was nice to see you again.' She stopped and cocked her head again. 'What's your name anyway?'

'Graham. Graham Pugh.'

'Well, Graham Pugh, see you around campus.' And she stood there with the door open until he got the message and left.

The room looked exactly like it had the last time Champion had been in it, except for the crime-scene seal on the door. He had another one in his car and he thought he'd go get it after he'd had a look around. The look around didn't take long. The blood was still on the bed and the floor on the vic's side of the room. The ceiling above still had cast-off. The roommate's bed was still stripped, with only a faint outline of the blood that had been found on it. If he hadn't seen it under luminol, he probably wouldn't realize it was there. If nothing else, the kid could clean, Champion thought. He began to poke around. He knew the crime-scene guys had gone over everything – the dresser drawers and the desk drawers – but he did so again, just in case something jumped out at him that the crime-scene guys hadn't recognized as important.

The Pugh kid's dresser top revealed a picture of his family and one of a Latina about the kid's age. He wondered if this was the one who left the blood on the kid's mattress. Checking the first drawer, he found underwear, socks, a jockstrap and a packet of condoms. The second drawer showed unfolded T-shirts and boxer briefs crushed in on top of workout clothes and some pants he didn't bother to hang up. Champion wondered if the fact that he was a slob with his clothes and so meticulous about cleaning his mattress meant anything. The last drawer held electronics – an iPad, a PlayStation III with a plastic tub full of games – and miscellany: books, hardback and paperback, used spiral notebooks, a catcher's mitt and a football.

The vic's dresser was much the same, except his electronics were more high-end and his miscellany was more in the form of expensive watches – three of them. Moving on to the vic's desk, he noted there was absolutely nothing on the top. He wondered if the crime-scene techs had taken anything and thought he better check that out. Opening the one drawer, he found a snapshot of the victim's parents during a loving moment, but not framed, a laptop, a spiral notebook and a Mont Blanc pen set. Not a Bic in sight.

On the Pugh kid's desk there was a coffee cup filled with pens, pencils, highlighters and a mean-looking letter opener. They had luminoled that, he knew. The desktop held several books on subjects Champion would rather not think about, stacked on one side. There was also a small collage of snapshots of the kid and his sisters and the kid and some male friends. Everybody was smiling. Nothing sinister at all. The drawer held newer spiral notebooks, several class syllabuses and a schedule of classes. Champion had to wonder if the kid was missing school.

There was a wall of closets and he opened the doors on both. In the vic's closet half the shirts and pants still had the tags on them with prices that boggled the mind. The other half – the ones hanging up, not the couple thrown carelessly on the floor of the closet – looked expensive. He figured the ones on the floor probably were too, but decided not to check out his suspicions. He could see the tips of several pairs of shoes sticking out beneath the pile of dirty clothes – three pair of expensive-looking running shoes and what looked like four pairs of leather dress shoes in different shades of brown.

The Pugh kid's closet held two cotton button-downs, one blue, the other yellow, one pair of blue jeans and two pairs of khakis. There was a tennis racket on the floor and one pair of shoes – the kind a kid his age would only wear to a job interview or church.

He shut the closet doors and made a one-eighty circle around the room. Nothing. It told him absolutely nothing. He decided to go down to his car, get that seal for the door, secure the letter opener in the glovebox then try old Gretchen Morley one more time.

I heard a noise coming from the room next door. Luna heard it too. We both turned toward Graham's room then looked back at each other. 'You go,' I said.

'No, you go,' she said. 'He's your son.'

'But he doesn't hate you,' I explained.

'Well, there is that,' Luna said and stood. 'If I'm not back in fifteen minutes, send food.'

I didn't laugh. Nothing about this was funny. She shrugged and headed out the door.

I heard her rap on Graham's door. Heard the door open and the sound of voices, no words distinguishable, then heard the door shut. Since Luna didn't come back, I had to assume she had been invited into his room. I moved closer to the wall that separated the two motel units and could make out the sounds of conversation. I could barely tell which one was talking and I definitely couldn't hear what they were saying. I thought about getting one of the glasses from the bathroom and pressing it against the wall, but having tried that before I knew it didn't really work. All I could do was wait.

I sat on my bed and thought about things. Things like how I was going to get my son out of this and what would happen if I couldn't. Did he do it? Definitely not. But could I prove it? The only way I knew how to do that was to find the person who *did* do it. Finally, the door to my room opened and both Luna and Graham came in.

'Hey, Mom,' he said.

I stood up but didn't run to him, as much as I wanted to. 'I'm sorry,' I said.

'No, it coulda happened the way you thought. But I found the girl. Ah, I didn't force her, Mom.' He turned red talking about it.

'I should have known you never would.'

He sank down on the bed Luna would be occupying later. 'Yeah, like you shoulda known I'd never sit up in my sleep and stare like a looney at my roommate?'

'We don't know that's true,' I said. 'Somebody told Champion that Bishop told that somebody you did that. We have no idea if Bishop was lying or if that somebody was lying.'

'I'm pretty sure I know who the somebody is,' Graham said.

'Yeah? Who?' I asked, just as Luna asked about the same thing.

'Gretchen Morley. Bishop's ex-girlfriend, the one who keyed his car. If Bishop told somebody that, then the person he would probably have told would have been Gretchen. And if he didn't tell her that, then she'd be the one most likely to make up something like that.'

'Why would she do that?' Luna asked.

'Because she's just as big a freak as Bishop was. Stone-cold crazy,' Graham said. 'A real looker but still loony tunes.'

'What about Bishop's best friend? Bobby Something?' I asked.

'Dunston, Mom. That's the third time I've told you that!'

'Don't get flip with me, young man!'

'Whatever,' he said, turning away from me.

'So what about Bobby *Dunston*?' I said, stressing the last name.

'What about him?' Graham countered.

'OK, you two. You're as bad as my two boys!' Luna said. 'Graham, just answer the question.'

'What was it?' he asked.

I sighed heavily. 'Could he have told Bobby Dunston instead of Gretchen?'

'Naw,' Graham said. 'Bishop used Bobby as more of an errand boy. You know, do this, do that. And Bobby did it. I don't think they had any deep discussions.'

'I still think we need to talk to him, and to Gretchen Morley,' I said. 'And probably that student adviser.'

'Gaylord Fuchs,' Graham said.

'Right,' I agreed. 'Can't believe I forgot *that* name.'

'Yeah, it *is* memorable,' Luna agreed.

Graham stood up. 'Fine. Let's do it. Bobby's on the second floor. We can stop there on our way to Gretchen's dorm.'

SIX

Champion stopped by the crime-scene lab to see if they'd taken anything off the vic's desktop.

Arridondo, a crime-scene tech, checked his notes. 'Nope. Nothing on top. Clean as a whistle.'

'Is that weird?' Champion asked.

Arridondo shrugged. 'I think everything about this kid is weird, but then, I don't like kids much.'

'Hell, I don't even like mine half the time,' Champion said. 'They're teenagers,' he said, which he figured explained it all. He thanked Arridondo and was on his way to check out the girlfriend – again.

Gretchen Morley was home the second time Champion knocked on her sorority room door. When she opened the door and saw him, her turquoise eyes got big and her full-lipped mouth puckered into a perfect 'O'. Champion dug a fingernail into the palm of his hand to keep his mind on business. Damn, he really needed to start dating.

'Need to ask you some more questions, Miss Morley. May I come in?' he asked.

'Oh, of course, Captain,' she said, backing into her room.

'That's detective, ma'am, not captain.'

'Oh!' she said again, then smiled a soft, 'I'm still in mourning' kind of smile.

Champion was afraid he was going to draw blood, he was digging so hard with his fingernails.

'I need to go over your statement about Graham Pugh and his behavior in the middle of the night,' he said.

'Excuse me?' she said, tilting her head so that her blonde tresses covered part of her face.

Champion looked away, then back and said, 'You told me that Bishop Alexander told you he'd wake up sometimes in the middle of the night and find Graham Pugh staring at him, and I quote, "If looks could kill . . ." End quote.'

'Um-hum,' she said. 'That's what Bish told me.'

'When did he tell you this?'

'When we were still dating.'

'Yes, but could you be more specific? Actually when?'

'You mean like the date? Gosh, I wouldn't know!' she said, her eyes big again and her mouth going for that 'O'.

Champion was beginning to think the girl was doing that on purpose. She absolutely knew the effect she had on him – on all men, he could only assume.

'You dated Bishop from when to when?' Champion asked, getting out his notebook so as not to have to look at her.

'Well, we started dating in October, right before Halloween. I remember because it was like our second date when we went to a Halloween party.' She smiled prettily. 'We went as Raggedy Ann and Andy.' Then she teared up and grabbed a Kleenex to dab at her eyes. 'It was such fun. We were so cute together!'

'And when did you stop dating?' he asked.

'Well, we decided to stop seeing each other right after we got back from Thanksgiving break.'

'It was a mutual decision to stop seeing each other?' Champion asked, looking at the girl.

'Oh, yes. It just wasn't, you know, working out.'

'Then why did you key his car and send him Ex-Lax brownies?'

She did the eyes and the 'O' again. He ignored it. Instead, he said, 'Miss Morley?'

'What?'

'I asked why, if it was a mutual parting of the ways, you felt the need to key his car – not once but twice – and send him Ex-Lax brownies.'

'I didn't do that.'

'Really?'

'Well, not really. I mean, I may have sent him some brownies after we stopped seeing each other, just one friend to another, but I certainly didn't put a laxative in them! That's just awful! If he got sick from those brownies, maybe he was allergic to nuts.' She brightened. 'Yes. I put nuts in those brownies! That must have been it.'

'Nut allergies, to my knowledge, don't cause diarrhoea. What about keying the car?'

'Oh, that was purely an accident! Really!'

'Twice?'

'Oh, no, it only happened once!' She smiled. He was beginning to see her tells. She smiled meant she lied. Big eyes and an 'O' also meant she lied. Maybe, he thought, just being awake meant she lied.

'Why did he dump you, Gretchen?' Champion asked.

Gretchen Morley burst into tears, sobbing like her heart would break. Having witnessed this performance before, he was wondering if maybe she was a theater major.

Bobby Dunston opened the door at the first knock. He was not an attractive young man. He was about my height, five foot and eleven inches, and probably weighed close to four hundred pounds. Even though he couldn't be more than nineteen or twenty, his hairline was receding, and to top all that off, he wore thick black-rimmed glasses and sported a nice crop of acne.

'Pugh!' he said on seeing Graham. 'What do *you* want?'

'Need to talk to you, Bobby,' Graham said.

'Well, I don't want to talk to you!' he said and started to slam the door.

Luna managed to put her size ten in the space before it closed. 'Police, Mr Dunston,' she said. 'We need to talk.'

Bobby let go of the door. 'If you're the police, why haven't you arrested *him*?' he said, pointing at Graham as he backed into the room.

It was a single room, half the size of Graham's, with only one twin-sized bed, one dresser and one desk. There was barely room for the three of us to join him.

'Sit down, Mr Dunston,' Luna said, her body language encouraging him to sink onto his bed. I let Luna have the one chair in the room while Graham and I held up walls. 'I need to ask you some questions about Bishop Alexander,' she said.

'Well, I can certainly tell you who killed him!' He looked at my son and pointed again. 'Him!'

'Jesus, Bobby! I didn't do shit!'

Luna waved a hand at Graham. 'Mr Dunston, do you have any specific reason for accusing Mr Pugh of this terrible crime?'

'What the hell was he doing while Bish was being stabbed to death, huh? Sleeping, for God's sake?' The young man began to cry. 'I mean, Bish never did anything to him but Bish said Pugh hated him and was always trying to do something to him!'

'Hey, wait a fuckin' min—' Graham started.

'Mr Pugh, please!' Luna said, shooting him a look.

I grabbed his arm and pulled him toward me. If I had to, I could muffle his next outburst.

'What kinds of things did Mr Alexander say Mr Pugh was trying to do?' Luna asked.

Dunston jumped up from the bed. 'Like he caught him going through his wallet—'

'I nev—' I clapped my hand over my son's mouth.

'And once Bish said he found dog crap in his bed! It was pretty obvious who did that!'

I could feel my son's tongue on my hand as he struggled to defend himself. I stepped on his foot – hard – and he stopped.

'And then there were the Ex-Lax brownies—'

'Um iffin naw!' Graham screamed from behind my hand.

'I understood from other sources that Mr Alexander's ex-girlfriend, Gretchen Morley, sent him those brownies. And keyed his car,' Luna said.

'Gretch would never do such a thing!' Bobby said. 'She loved Bish! She planned on marrying him!'

'I thought they broke up?' Luna asked.

He shook his head. 'No, not at all. They were just taking a break. Couples do that all the time.'

'Is that what Mr Alexander told you?' Luna asked.

'Well, he never went into detail about the break. Gretch told me.'

'Did you ask him about it?'

'Oh, no!' Bobby Dunston said, sitting back down on his bed. 'You know guys don't discuss their relationships. It's just not something we do,' he said, a smirky kind of smile on his face.

'Really?' Luna asked.

'Oh, yes! You know, we talk about sports, and hunting and fishing, and about schoolwork, some but not much, and, well, we do talk about the women on campus.' He smirked again. 'You know, the ones you want to – well—'

'I get your drift,' Luna said. 'And did Mr Alexander want to you-know-what with a lot of different girls?'

Bobby Dunston laughed. 'Oh, yes! He had his pick on campus!'

'Even after he started dating Miss Morley?'

'Ah, well, I don't know,' he said, looking down at the floor.

'Surely he'd tell you if he was having sex with other girls. That's what you said you two talked about. Not relationships but meaningless sex, right?'

'Ah . . .'

'So was he having meaningless sex with other women while he was having a relationship with Miss Morley?' Luna pushed.

'Ah, well, maybe.'

'Maybe?'

'Girls were always all over him!' Bobby said, jumping up from the bed again. 'It wasn't Bish's fault! You know, a guy can't always control himself when it's just out there like that!'

'Do you know of any specific women?' Luna asked.

'Well, I know one he didn't bang. Excuse me – have sex with.'

'And who would that be?'

'This girl Lexie Thurgood. She lives right down the hall from Bish. She threw herself at him a bunch but he always just laughed at her. I mean, she's like seven feet tall or something.'

Luna and I, both close to six foot, took umbrage at that remark. But she was able to control herself. I, unfortunately, let my hand slip from Graham's mouth.

'You monumental fuck-up!' Graham shouted and headed for the bed on which Bobby Dunston sat. Bobby jumped up as Luna grabbed my son's arm.

'Pugh, I'm going to make you leave the room if you can't control yourself!' she said between clenched teeth.

'But all that he's saying is bullshit! If Bishop told him that then he was lying through his teeth!'

'Bish never lied to me!' Dunston claimed.

'Again, bullshit! Bishop lied to everyone, especially you! He kept you around as a yes man, somebody to wipe his ass—'

'He did not!' Dunston shouted, lumbering toward Graham.

Luna managed to get herself between my son and the four-hundred-pound yes man. 'Enough!' she shouted, one hand on each boy's chest. 'Mrs Pugh, please take your son out of the room.'

'Oh, you brought your mommy?' Bobby Dunston smirked. 'You're not going to the principal's office, Pugh! You're getting the needle!'

Graham lunged for Bobby while Bobby lunged back. I got Graham around the waist and hauled him out the door. I'm not sure what Luna did with Dunston but I kind of wished for some bruises.

She met us in the hallway a few minutes later. She punched Graham in the shoulder. 'Hey!' Graham said, frowning and fisting his hands.

'Listen up, kid!' Luna said, anger sounding in her voice. 'You are out of this if you do anything like that again! You got it?'

'But he—'

'I don't care if he crapped in your oatmeal! You don't talk! You don't say shit! Do you understand me?'

'But—' Graham started but I interrupted.

'He understands,' I said, slapping my son on the back of the head. 'Right?' I asked him.

He sighed. 'Yeah. Right. Whatever.'

'We're going to the girlfriend's room next. If you so much as sneeze, you'll be in the hall, got it?'

'I said I did!' Graham said. 'Jeez!'

We all stared at each other, let out almost simultaneous deep sighs and headed out of McMillan Hall on our way to Gretchen Morley's sorority house.

*   *   *

Champion knew the girl was lying. There was no doubt about that. But what exactly was she lying about? What she claimed Bishop Alexander said to her about the Pugh kid? Or just the crap about the break-up and her supposed innocence when it came to the keying of the vic's car and the Ex-Lax brownies? Or maybe everything. It wasn't the first time he'd had the fantasy of picking a witness or suspect up by the heels and shaking them like a piggy bank until all the truth, like dimes and nickels, came falling out.

He was about to call it quits and head back to the station when there was a knock on the girl's door. As she was still sobbing her little heart out, Champion said, 'Want me to get that?'

She replied by nodding several times without stopping the sobs. Champion got up and opened the door. He was shocked but not exactly surprised to see Elena Luna, the Pugh kid and his mom standing there. 'Well, Elena, I see you made it. Didn't expect to see you right here, though.'

'Sorry, Nate. Didn't mean to butt in. We just wanted to talk to Gretchen Morley for a minute. We can come back later,' Elena said, taking the two Pughs by an arm each and preparing to lead them away.

'No, no. You're here. Come on in. Maybe y'all have some questions I didn't think to ask,' he said, smiling what he considered his best smile. Others often deemed it his shark-like smile.

The two women looked at each other – as if looking for signals – then slowly walked in the room, the kid trailing behind.

Gretchen looked up. 'O-M-G!' she said. 'What is *he* doing here?'

'People actually say that?' Luna asked the mom. 'In initials?' The mom didn't answer.

'Miss Morley, this is Detective Elena Luna from another jurisdiction. She's here as a consultant. Could you answer her questions, please?'

Gretchen looked from one to the other of them, studying each face. 'No. I don't think so. I think I want a lawyer.'

'That's your prerogative, Miss Morley,' Champion said, 'but

once you have an attorney then we can no longer help you in any way. I'm afraid I'll have to treat you as a suspect after that.'

'A suspect?' she screeched, jumping up and dropping used Kleenex all over the floor. 'How can you say that? Bish was my . . . my friend!'

'I'm sorry, Miss Morley, that's just the way this thing works. If you have an attorney representing you then we must go on the assumption that you have something to hide and are therefore a viable suspect in our investigation.'

The girl sank back down on her bed. 'I'm not a suspect!' she whined. 'I'm not!'

'Do you want to answer some questions now or do you want to call your attorney?'

Champion noticed that her eyes weren't red like someone who had been sobbing her heart out only moments before. He had to admit he hadn't seen any actual tears. So maybe not a theater major – maybe just another sociopath. He'd met so many in his career they were becoming boring.

Gretchen sighed. 'Whatever,' she said. 'Ask away.' She leaned back against the wall, her legs stretched out before her across the width of the bed, arms folded across her chest. Champion figured this wasn't going to go very far.

'Detective Luna,' he said, his arm outstretched toward Gretchen Morley. 'The floor is yours.'

Luna shot him a look that he decided wasn't one hundred percent friendly and said, 'Miss Morley, I know you're grieving and I hate to disturb you, but I do have a few questions.'

'Whatever,' the younger woman said.

'I have concerns about the purported Ex-Lax brownies and the keying of the victim's car,' Luna said.

Gretchen sighed. 'I already told him,' she said, pointing at Champion. 'I didn't do it. I think he was allergic to the nuts I put in the brownies. There certainly was no laxative in them, for heaven's sake! And as for keying his car, it was an accident.' She looked up quickly and said, 'I only did it once. If it happened again, it was somebody else. Maybe him!' she said, pointing at Graham.

'I nev—'

Luna shot him a look and Graham clamped his mouth shut. But then he moved forward and whispered something in Luna's ear. Luna nodded her head and looked back at Gretchen.

'According to his roommate, there were no nuts in those brownies,' she said.

'Well, he *would* lie, wouldn't he?'

'I understand someone actually saw you purposely key the victim's car,' Luna said.

Gretchen Morley jumped up from her bed. 'Did *he* say that?' she asked, pointing at Graham. 'Because it's a lie! He wasn't even in town when I—' She stopped herself, then said, 'When that happened.'

'No, Graham Pugh is not the witness,' Luna said.

The young woman fell back on the bed, crossing her arms over her chest. Champion decided the pout on her face was definitely losing its appeal. 'Well, whoever! They're lying!'

'Seems everybody but you lies, is that it, Miss Morley?' Champion cut in.

'Well, I don't know about everybody,' she said, sitting up straight with her hands on her hips, 'but somebody sure as shit is!'

Champion looked at Luna. 'Do you have any more questions, Detective?' he asked.

'No, I think I'm through with this one for the moment, Detective,' she said. 'But I may need to talk with you again, Miss Morley, after I've had time to confer with Detective Champion and the other witnesses.'

'What other witnesses?' Gretchen yelled, jumping up.

'Thank you for your time, Miss Morley,' Luna said and ushered the kid and his mom out of the room, Champion following behind.

Once outside the sorority house, Champion asked, 'OK, so who said they saw her key the vic's car?'

Luna shrugged. 'Me. I lied.'

'Damn,' he said. 'I was hoping . . .'

'We did talk to the vic's bestie, Bobby—'

'Dunston,' Graham supplied with a sigh.

'Right. Bobby Dunston,' Luna said. 'And he reported that some girl named . . .?' She looked at Graham to fill in the blank.

Again, he sighed. 'Lexie Thurgood. Why don't you write these things down?'

'Hush,' Luna said to him and turned to Champion. 'What he said.'

'Yeah, Lexie Thurgood. I already talked to her. Lives in his' – he said, pointing at Graham – 'building. Tall chick. Overheard a fight between him' – again pointing at Graham – 'and the vic.'

'So she's the—' Graham started but Luna interrupted.

'Shut up,' she said.

'So what did this Bobby say about Lexie?' Champion asked.

'That she came onto the vic repeatedly and the vic shot her down in public.'

Champion and Luna both noticed at the same time that Graham's arm was in the air and he was waving it about.

'What?' Luna said.

Graham lowered his arm. 'I wouldn't put a lot of stock in anything Bobby says. He was so far up Bishop's ass he couldn't see daylight. And there's Fuchs!' he said, obviously getting excited.

'Fuchs?' Champion said, raising an eyebrow.

'Gaylord Fuchs,' the mom said. 'Bishop's student adviser. There was some drama with Fuchs' wife and he took a swing at Bishop.'

'And missed!' the kid added.

Champion drew Luna away from the mother and son and said softly, 'You know, Elena, I'm not real comfortable having these two tag along. The kid's my prime suspect, you know.'

'I know you think so,' Luna said, also speaking softly, 'but it's crap. Looks to me like that little twat we just talked to had more reason than anybody to do in the vic.'

'I'm not saying you're wrong on that count but I need to follow-up on the information you just gave me about Lexie

Thurgood and that Fuchs guy. I don't mind you coming along. But not them.'

Luna nodded her head. 'OK, we can deal with that,' she said, left him and walked over to mother and son.

SEVEN

'Did you ever hear Lexie come on to Bishop?' I asked my son. As we'd come on this mission in Luna's car, we took the U.T. shuttle back to the motel and were now in his room discussing things.

He shook his head. 'No. Like I said, anything Bobby Dunston says is probably a load of crap.'

'How well do you know Lexie?' I asked.

Graham shrugged. 'I see her around. She lives just down the hall. I mean, we say hey and crap but that's about it.'

'What do you think she told Champion about your fight with Bishop?'

Again, the shrug. 'Hell if I know. I don't even know which fight she supposedly witnessed. I mean, the way we'd go off on each other, it could have been anything.'

'Did you ever strike him?' I asked.

'Jeez, Mom! No! I told you that already! We yelled at each other but mainly because he kept accusing me of shit! The guy was an asshole.'

'I think we've already determined that,' I said. 'But did you ever fight in the hall or anywhere else public about anything that could be construed as threatening?'

'Construed as threatening.' He grinned. 'Nice turn of phrase, Mom.'

'Hey, I'm a writer. Words are my life. Answer the question.'

He shrugged again and I wanted to put my hand firmly on his shoulder to keep him from doing it, but I restrained myself. 'We fought. About crap, mostly. I mean, did I ever threaten his life? Not that I recall. Did I ever threaten to punch his lights out? Probably.'

I sighed. 'I wonder what Lexie Thurgood is telling them now,' I said, mostly to myself.

* * *

Luna noted that Lexie Thurgood was not seven feet tall. She was, however, several inches above Luna's own five eleven and a half. After introductions were made, Luna smiled at the young woman and asked, 'You play for the Lady Horns?'

'No, not me. I tried out for basketball in middle school and got cut from the team.' She raised one very large foot. 'I have a tendency to trip over these,' she said. 'Even walking, much less running.' She grinned. 'I'm a fairly amazing klutz.'

'Why don't we all take a seat?' Champion said, shooting Luna a disapproving look. She wondered if the Austin PD wasn't into putting witnesses and suspects at ease as a way to ferret out information. She'd have to tell him how to do it. Obviously he didn't watch cop shows on TV.

They all took seats, Lexie on the bed and Champion and Luna in the two desk chairs. 'We've got some rather personal questions, Miss Thurgood,' Champion said. 'I hope you don't mind.'

The young woman spread her arms wide. 'Hey, I'm an open book. Ask away.'

'We've been told by reliable sources that Bishop Alexander embarrassed you in front of other people,' Champion said. 'Is that true?'

'Probably,' she said. 'Bish was always doing something to humiliate or embarrass somebody. He was a real shit.'

'We heard from our source that you came onto him and he shot you down,' Luna said, going for shock value.

'Oh, yeah! I forgot about that. Early last semester I asked him if he'd like to go to a dance with me. It was the old Sadie Hawkins crap. Can't believe they still do that. But the girls are supposed to ask the guys and I thought he was cute.' She laughed. 'And he said, "With you, Gigantor?" Pissed me off at the time but I got over it. I've been called worse. Besides, I'm in a relationship now and whether or not Bishop Alexander found me attractive is beside the point. My guy thinks I'm hot.' She grinned.

'Was that the only time he made fun of you?' Luna asked.

'Oh, God, no. He'd see me in the hall – here or in a building on campus, or even walking the mall – and if somebody was with him, and there usually was, he'd say something really original like, "How's the weather up there?" or something equally asinine.'

'And if he was alone?' Champion prodded.

'Not a word,' Lexie said. 'He needed an audience. Actually, he avoided eye contact when he was alone. I think I scared him,' she said and grinned again.

Luna couldn't help thinking about the men in her life who'd seemed threatened by her. There's just something about a big woman that many men found intimidating. She, obviously like Lexie Thurgood, had often used it to her own advantage.

'I shared with Detective Luna your account of the fight between Graham Pugh and Bishop Alexander that you witnessed,' Champion said. 'Have you thought of anything you could add to that?'

Lexie shook her head. 'Not really. I mean, I don't know Graham well but he seems like a nice guy. Can't imagine him doing anything like what happened to Bishop, but who else could have done it? I mean, he was killed in the middle of the night, right? And Graham just slept through it?' She shook her head. 'Weird. But, you know, Bishop was a creep to me and I barely knew him. I can only imagine how bad Graham had it, living in the same room with him. You know, you could ask that ass-kissing sycophant who was always trailing after Bishop. Bobby—'

'Dunston,' Luna supplied.

'Right. Bobby Dunston. He'd know more about the relation-ship between Graham and Bishop than me. Of course, he'd be a good suspect, too!' she said, seeming to get excited. 'I mean, Bishop treated him horribly! Made fun of him in front of anyone at any time! Someone even told me that Bishop called him a name in front of Bobby's parents! Can you believe that?'

'Who told you that?' Champion asked.

Lexie Thurgood stopped for a moment, obviously lost in thought. Finally, she said, 'I dunno, where did I hear that?' She shrugged. 'It was right before the winter break, I know that. 'Cause I wondered if Bobby's parents would make him stop running with Bishop after that. But who?' Lost in thought again, she finally snapped her fingers. 'Brittany! I don't know her last name. She was in my economics class. She told me about it because she was around once when Bishop said something he thought was funny to me. She thought I'd like to know.' She grinned. 'And of course I did!'

'Where can we find this Brittany?' Champion asked, writing the name down in his notebook.

'Like I said, she was in my economics class last semester. Tuesday nights, six-thirty to nine o'clock with Professor Winston, but he was never there. We always had a T.A. But if you need to ask the registrar about it, you need to say Professor Winston.'

Champion stood up and Luna followed his lead. 'Thanks, Miss Thurgood, we appreciate your help.'

Both detectives shook the girl's hand before leaving the room. Once in the elevator on the way down to the first floor, Champion asked Luna, 'So, what did you think?'

'I think she was believable. Didn't seem to be hiding anything,' Luna said.

'Yeah, that's what I thought about Morley the first time I interviewed her.'

Luna grinned. 'You sure you weren't just swayed by her pouty mouth and perky breasts?'

'I resent that remark,' Champion said, looking at Luna with a tiny bit of lust in his heart.

The minute Graham's mom left his room he grabbed his keys and headed to his car, and then straight to the B&B dorm and Miranda Wisher's room. She wasn't there. Coming back down the stairs, he looked into the living room of the dorm where Miranda was standing with another girl, talking. He gingerly went up to her.

'Hey, Miranda,' he said. 'Got a minute?'

She turned slowly and looked at him. 'I'm sort of in the middle of something right now.'

'Then I'll just wait over here,' he said and headed to a gold-embroidered sofa where he flung himself down. Both the young women, Miranda and the one she was talking to, looked at him, then away, continuing their conversation. Graham got the distinct impression it was going on a lot longer than it would have had he not been sitting there waiting.

Finally, the woman Miranda was talking to looked over at him, then back at Miranda, smiled at her, patted her arm, turned and left. Graham stood up from the sofa but didn't move toward Miranda. She glanced over at him, sighed deeply then walked toward him.

'What do you want? I told you to give the police my number, but I haven't heard from them.'

'I don't care about the police or if they talk to you. Probably won't make much of a difference. The guy in charge seems to like me a lot for it.' Graham shook his head. 'But that's not why I'm here.' He cleared his throat and said, 'I'm sorry. Really sorry. I should have looked for you, I know that. But the whole thing was like a fog. I knew it had happened but I didn't know who with or where we met and – and I'm sorry. I'm an asshole.'

'Yeah, you are that,' Miranda said. She cocked her head and looked him over. 'But a very cute asshole. And,' she said, still studying him intently, 'I wasn't so drunk that I couldn't make a rational decision. I knew you were drunk but I guess I didn't realize how drunk. Besides, I liked you. I liked the things you said when we talked, and, like I said,' she added with a grin, 'you *are* a cute asshole.'

'So you're not mad at me anymore?' Graham asked.

'Would it matter if I was?' she asked.

Graham nodded. 'Yeah, for some reason it really would matter.'

'Don't worry. I'm not going to talk you down to other girls or anything. Your rep should still be solid – if it ever was.'

'Yeah, I don't know about that. Now that I'm being accused of murder—'

She laughed. 'There are girls around campus who will find that immensely attractive.'

'Yeah, well, they're not the girls I want to impress,' Graham said.

She cocked her head. 'Are you flirting with me?' she asked.

'Jeez, you don't let up, do you?'

'Well, are you?'

Graham sighed. 'I'm trying to. How'm I doing?'

She held a thumb in the 'up' position. 'Better than earlier.'

'So, you know, maybe,' Graham started, clearing his throat again, 'you know, if I don't get arrested any time soon, we could, ah—'

'Are you asking me out on a date or do you just want to get laid? I mean, either's OK, I just need to know.'

Graham could feel himself turning red. 'A date,' he said quickly. 'Just a date.'

She nodded. 'I think that would be best. But I don't want to wait to see if you get arrested. Tell me first – did you kill your roommate?'

'God, no!'

'Good,' Miranda said. 'Then let's you and me prove it, OK?'

I wasn't used to sitting around twiddling my thumbs. I should have been with Luna, asking questions, but no, here I was, stuck in a godforsaken motel room doing nothing but staring at the door, waiting for Luna to show up. Graham was in his room next door and I could hear the TV. He obviously wasn't studying, which I was pretty sure meant bye-bye to this semester. While I was pondering all this, my phone rang. Hoping it was Luna with some news, I grabbed the phone but the screen informed me it was my husband. I tried to sound interested.

'Hey,' I said.

'What's wrong?' he asked. Obviously my try at sounding interested hadn't worked.

'What's not wrong?' I sighed. 'I'm stuck in this stinking motel room, Graham's wasting away watching TV – probably cartoons if I know my son – and Luna's out and about with that Champion guy interviewing suspects and asking questions and—'

'And she won't let you come along,' Willis finished for me.

'Not so much her, I think, as that asshole Champion. He still thinks Graham is his best suspect!'

'They don't have any others?'

'Well, Bishop's ex-girlfriend looks good – to me, at least, and to Luna, too, I think. And then there's Bishop's BFF and his student adviser. It seems like Graham's roommate was a real piece of work, as bad as Graham said he was. He put down this boy Bobby in front of other people all the time and hit on the adviser's wife. But,' I said and sighed, remembering how Bobby Dunston seemed so smitten with Bishop, 'I doubt the kid would have had the balls to stab Bishop over and over.'

'What about the student adviser?' Willis asked.

'We haven't met him yet. I don't know if Luna and Champion are going to interview him today or not.'

'Well, don't go letting people off the hook like the BFF,' Willis said. 'Every port in a storm.'

'I agree. Bobby gave Luna and Champion another name, a girl who Bishop put down in public. They went to see her but told Graham and me, essentially, to get lost.'

'Keep me posted – on anything. Anything at all,' Willis said.

'I will, honey, I promise. Meanwhile, what's going on at home?'

'Oh, hey, I got that contract with Weaver!'

'Weaver?'

'The guy I had breakfast with the morning this shit-storm started,' he said.

'I thought he said no.'

'He did. But when Weaver did his due diligence, the lowest bidder turned out to be a flake who'd screwed up a couple of high-profile projects. So I was next lowest.'

'Not too low, I hope.'

'We won't be eating beans for the foreseeable future but filet mignon's not in our future either.'

'Right smack dab in the middle, huh?' I said.

'As usual.'

'I'll make sure my next book is twice as long.'

'Think they'll pay twice as much?' he asked, and I could hear the grin in his voice. It was a good thing to hear at this point in time.

'No, but I'm thinking of a real bodice ripper. Maybe my agent can take it to another publisher.'

'When you get home we can practice some of the scenes,' he said, which made me laugh.

'You try tearing my clothes, buddy, and I'll max out the Visa!' Changing the subject, I asked, 'How are the girls?'

'Bess and Alicia are trying their damnedest to keep Megan from telling anyone who'll listen all about her brother the serial killer.'

'That girl! Where's your duct tape?'

'Not a bad idea. At least it might work as a threat,' he said.

'Well, if you need any more torture techniques, just give me a call,' I said.

He sighed. 'Try to stay upbeat, honey. This too shall pass.'

'I'll try. And call often. It helps.'

'I'll do that,' he said. We both said 'I love you' and that was the end of the conversation.

And I sat back on the bed, my legs outstretched, pillows propping me up against the headboard and stared at the door, waiting for Luna to show up.

'Why didn't Graham wake up?' Luna asked me.

'Because he sleeps like the dead— Sorry, bad choice of words.'

'But his alarm wakes him, right?'

'So? What are you getting at, Luna?' I asked, my mama dander heating up.

'It had to be noisy. You can't stab someone repeatedly without a sound. You'd think the vic would scream, at least with the first thrust,' she said. 'And there had to be, well, you know, noise.'

'What are you implying?'

Luna sighed. 'I'm not implying shit, Pugh! I'm just stating a fact: Graham didn't wake up. Why not?'

'I don't know!' I shouted. 'He's a sound sleeper!'

'Bullshit!' she shouted back. 'Nobody could sleep through what was happening in that room!'

'You don't know that! Are you accusing Graham—'

Luna sank down on her bed. 'No, Pugh, I'm not accusing

Graham of anything. It's a legitimate question: why didn't he wake up? And my thoughts tend to wander to questions like: did he eat or drink anything before he went to bed? Could someone have slipped him a mickey?'

'No one does that anymore,' I said. 'It would have to have been one of those date-rape drugs.'

'A mickey's a mickey,' she said. 'Whatever is used. That's not the point.'

I stood up and walked to the wall between my motel room and Graham's and rapped sharply on it. 'What?' came my son's disembodied voice.

'Come here!' I shouted through the wall.

'Why?' he shouted back.

'Because I said so!' Boy, I hadn't used that line in a long time.

'Whatever,' was his reply, but it was barely audible.

Within a minute he was banging on the door. I opened it to let him in. 'What?' he said in a surly manner.

'Watch your attitude!' I said.

'Why? You think somebody's going to suspect me of murder because I have a lousy attitude?'

'No, because you're going to get through this, and when you come out the other side you don't want me to snatch you bald-headed! That's why!'

He flung himself down on my bed, his long body taking up most of it. I butt-scooched Luna over and sat next to her on her bed. 'Did you eat or drink anything when you got to the dorm Sunday night?' I asked.

'What?' he asked, anger and confusion warring on his features.

'Did. You. Eat. Or. Drink—'

'I heard you!' he said. I swear I was going to do more than snatch him bald-headed when this was over. 'Yeah, I went down to the cafeteria. Had some curly fries and a Coke. So sue me!'

'Was the Coke a bottle or a can, or fountain?' Luna asked.

'Fountain,' Graham said. 'Why?'

'Were the items ever out of your sight?' she asked.

'What? No! I mean—' He thought for a moment, then said,

'Well, yeah, I forgot to get a napkin and I left the fries and my Coke on the table when I went to get it.'

'Was there anyone else in the cafeteria?' Luna asked.

'Yeah. Lots of people. The day before the new semester, it was crowded as hell.'

'Anyone you knew?' Luna asked.

Graham shrugged. 'I don't know. Probably. I've been in that dorm since freshman year so I know a lot of people there. But I don't remember anyone specifically. What are you getting at? You think someone doctored my food?'

'I'm just wondering how you could have slept through the commotion of Bishop being stabbed to death only a few feet away from you,' Luna said.

Graham's handsome face turned ugly. 'You mean, if I didn't do it, right?'

Luna reached out a hand and touched Graham's outstretched leg. 'Hon, I know you didn't do it. I'm just trying to prove you didn't do it. Did you feel groggy when you got up the next morning?'

He shrugged. 'No groggier than usual, I think. I mean, I'm not exactly a morning person, and this was like six something and I just don't do six anything.'

'What time did you go to bed?' I asked.

'Early. Well, earlyish, for me anyway. I got stuck with that seven o'clock class so I went to bed around ten, ten-thirty. I was pretty sleepy anyway, what with driving—'

He stopped and looked from me to Luna and back again. 'Yeah, I was really sleepy. Driving an hour doesn't usually do that to me.' He sat up. 'You think that's it? You think somebody dosed me? So I wouldn't wake up while they were killing Bishop? Jesus!' He hugged himself. 'That really sucks!'

'Better you slept through it,' Luna said. 'The alternative isn't pretty.'

Graham and I made eye contact; I wasn't sure about him but I was about to vomit.

Champion was glad to have gotten rid of Elena, if only for a little bit. She'd gone back to the motel room she shared with the kid's mother and he was free to contact the administration office and find out who this Brittany person was who told Lexie Thurgood about Bishop Alexander putting down Bobby Dunston in front of Bobby's parents. 'Jeez, what a mouthful,' he thought aloud. As a parent himself, he could only imagine what he'd do if some asshole kid said something nasty about his son or daughter in front of him. He *did* carry a gun.

The woman on the other end of the line in the admin office told him he'd have to come in and show his credentials before she could give out any information. And he'd better hurry since they closed at four. It was fifteen minutes to four when he left Luna behind.

He hustled over to the building that housed so much of the business of the university, a squat, square building that looked like it had been built back in the unimaginative sixties.

The woman he'd talked to on the phone said he needed to talk to the T.A. assigned to most of Professor Winston's classes, Tina Ng, whom she said should be in that same room right now, setting up for another class. She gave him the building and the number of the room.

'Oh,' he said, 'while I have you, could you tell me where I can find a student adviser named Gaylord Fuchs?'

She hit some buttons on her computer and looked up. 'He has an office in this building, fourth floor, but his hours are ten to one.' Looking again at the screen, she said, 'He's a teaching assistant. And he has classes from one-thirty to three-thirty, but I'm sure he's already on his way home.'

'Can you give me his home address?' Champion asked.

The woman sighed and read out a number and a street. Champion had a vague idea where that was. He thanked her and headed out, hoping to get some information from the T.A., Ng, before class started.

The young T.A. was in the room, setting up a projector when he walked in. It didn't look like a room to him, more a large auditorium. It looked like it seated at least one hundred, and he was surprised that a T.A. would be responsible for a class that size. Knowing that Ng was a Vietnamese name, he wasn't surprised to see the back of a small, dark-haired young woman.

'Miss Ng?' he asked.

She turned toward him. Her hair was cut in a stark, blunt cut and she wore glasses with heavy frames and lenses. Her body and face put her at about the age of fourteen, but he doubted that could be true.

'Yes?' she said.

He showed her his credentials and got straight to the point. 'I need to interview a young woman who was in one of your classes last semester. All I have is her first name, Brittany, but she was in the Tuesday night six-thirty to nine p.m. class.'

She didn't say anything for what felt like quite a long time to Champion. Finally, he said, 'Miss Ng?'

'Yes?'

'Do you speak English?' He was unsure if she'd understood what he'd asked.

'As well as most Californians,' she said. 'Sorry, I'm just trying to think. Brittany.' She was quiet another moment. 'I can't think of one offhand. I'd have to look that up.'

She finished her sentence and stood staring at him. Finally, he said, 'Can you do that, please? Go look it up?'

'I have a class starting and last semester's rolls have already gone to Records,' she said.

'When do you think you could find that for me?' Champion asked.

'I can't,' she said.

'You just said—' Champion started, beginning to get a little frustrated.

'But you could probably get someone in admin to do it.'

'Probably?'

Tina Ng shrugged. 'It could happen. But then again—'

'I really need this information,' Champion said between clenched teeth.

'Then maybe you should get a, you know, warrant or something? Admin would probably appreciate that.' She looked beyond him as sounds indicated students entering the hall. 'Gotta go,' she said and turned away from him.

Champion didn't like the feeling of being dismissed but figured there wasn't much he could do about it. The thought crossed his mind that maybe he could arrest her, but thinking about all the paperwork involved stifled that urge. He turned and exited the building.

'So when are you supposed to see Champion again?' I asked Luna.

She shrugged. 'Don't know. We didn't set up a time or anything,' she said.

'Maybe you should call him?' I asked.

'Why? You got something on your mind?'

'You said he got another name from that Lexie person. Somebody who told y'all that Bishop put Bobby down in front of his parents, right?'

'Right.'

'Who told her that?' I asked.

She shrugged. 'She only had a first name. Beth, Bethany, something with a "B." Nate said he'd follow up on it.'

'I can't believe you call him by his first name,' I said, slightly miffed that she was getting familiar with the enemy.

'Hey, I've known the guy for years. We're on a first-name basis – which, when you think about it, you and I are not.'

'What's that supposed to mean?' I asked her, getting a little heated.

'Just an observation,' she said.

'So you're on his side?' I all but shouted.

'God, Pugh! Lighten up! There's no side. There's only finding out who killed that brat of a kid. Actually, I'm a little surprised it took this long for somebody to kill him.'

'I can't lighten up!' I said. 'My son's future is on the line.'

'I'm not going to let anything happen to Graham. I guaran-damn-tee you that. It would just behoove us to find out who killed that little asshole as quickly as possible.'

'Behoove?'

'It's a word! Look it up!'

'I know it's a word. It's just not a word one hears that often.'

'*One* hears?'

'Just trying to stay in the moment. You started it,' I said.

'Going forward,' she said, glaring at me, 'I don't think Bobby Dunston has the wherewithal to do old Bishy-boy in.

But I'm wondering about his parents. I mean, we need to know what Bishop said about their son in front of them. And what kind of people they are.'

'Overweight, going by their son,' I said.

'You're such a bigot,' she said.

'Am not,' I said.

'Are too,' she said.

'Moving on . . .'

'I don't think their physical appearance has anything to do with it. Are they the kind of people who'd get so pissed they'd off the vic? That's the question.'

'Don't you think Graham would have noticed if a parent was hanging around the cafeteria?'

'I've taken both my boys back to school and helped them move back in the dorm. And I've eaten in the cafeteria before driving home. There were lots of other parents doing the same.'

I sighed. 'Point taken.' I thought for a moment. 'OK, then. We need to look into Mr and Mrs Dunston. But I'm still putting my money on Gretchen Morley.'

'Jeez, she's a piece of work, huh? Can't figure out if she's just a bad actress or a pathological liar.'

'Same thing, right?'

'There you go again, parading around your prejudices.'

'And you're not prejudiced against pathological liars?'

'It was the bad actress part I was referring to. People can't help it if they can't act. I mean, you're no Meryl Streep yourself,' she said.

'Why do we keep getting off the subject?' I asked.

'What subject?'

'We're listing suspects, dumbass! We've got the Dunstons, possibly Bobby as well, and Gretchen. Who else?'

'Maybe Lexie Thurgood. I mean, I don't think so but she might be a really *good* actress.'

'Oh!' I said, lightbulb in my head. 'That guy Fuchs!'

'We need to interview him,' Luna said.

'Right!' I said, jumping up. 'Let's go!'

She gave me a look. 'I meant Champion and I need to interview him. Not you.'

'This is giving me a headache,' I said.

'Should we call room service for some soothing cocktails?' Luna asked.

'If only,' I said and sighed. Why motels don't have that service, I'll never know.

EIGHT

I got up early the next morning to encourage Graham to try to go to class. It was Wednesday and he still had that seven a.m. class.

'I'm gonna drop it,' he said and rolled over in bed, his back to me.

'No, you're not!' I said, poking him in the ribs.

'Jeez, Mom! That was bad enough when I was in high school! I'm an adult! Stop it!'

'You're not an adult,' I said. 'You're only twenty. You're not an adult until you're twenty-one.'

At that comment he turned and sat up in bed. 'You mean to say I can vote *and* die for my country but unless I'm old enough to legally buy booze I'm not an adult?'

OK, so sometimes my values shift around a bit. 'Fine,' I said, turning toward the door. 'Drop the course. But I thought you needed it to meet your majority requirements. If you want to try to do it next year, and forget about some of those easy classes you were going to take—'

'OK, OK!' he said, swinging his legs over the side of the bed. 'I'm getting up. But you'd better leave, I'm semi-naked here.'

'Fine!' I said and headed for the door.

'Fine!' he shot back, but I was almost out and decided to ignore him.

Back in the room I shared with Luna, she was sitting up on the side of her bed, phone to her ear. At first, thinking she might be talking to Champion, I was anxious. Then I noticed the phone she had to her ear was mine. She said, 'Hold on a minute,' and held the phone out to me. 'It's your prettier half,' she said and fell back in the bed.

'Have you called Champion yet?' I asked, taking the phone from her hand.

'Jesus, Pugh, it's not even seven!'

I shrugged – having forgotten that fact – and put the phone to my ear. 'Hey, honey,' I said.

'Hey, your ownself, and tell Luna thanks for the compliment. I have to agree, I've always felt I was prettier than you.'

'You know I'll get you for that, right?'

'I'm hoping the aging process will have blurred your memory and you'll forget about it by the time you get home.'

'That's two,' I said.

'Only two?'

'Did you call for a reason?' I asked.

'Just want to see what's going on,' he said.

I sat down on my bed. 'Not much change since yesterday. Hopefully we'll find out something from that cop friend of Luna's sometime today. If she ever calls him.'

'She's right, babe, it's still only a little after seven.'

'Her being right's not the point,' I said.

'Then what is?' he asked.

'The point is I'm mad, I'm frustrated and I'm scared! And I don't like this crap!'

'Deep breaths, babe.'

'Don't try to placate me!' I all but shouted.

He sighed. 'Fine, go ahead. Take it out on me. Better me than the cop who wants to arrest our son.'

I sighed myself. 'Shut up,' I said, my voice quiet.

'You shut up,' he said, just as quiet.

'Willis—'

'Yeah, babe?'

'Can you come here?'

Again with the sigh. 'Babe, I just signed a contract with Weaver. I can't. Not until—'

'Don't say it,' I said.

'If you *really* need me there, I'll come,' he said.

I took a deep breath – like he'd suggested earlier. 'No, not now. I hope this will play out soon. They've got to figure out a better suspect than Graham. Did I tell you we worked out Graham was probably roofied?'

'No shit?'

'That's what we're thinking,' I said.

'Any way to prove it?' he asked.

'Whatever it was probably already went through his system so there's no way to tell at this point.'

Willis was quiet for a moment. Finally, he said, 'You know, whoever did this, when I find them, I think I'll have to do something physical.'

'You don't do physical,' I said.

'Usually, no. But whoever did this is setting Graham up for the fall, and, you know, hacking up old Bishop's one thing but don't blame it on someone else.'

I almost laughed. 'Because they should just man up and admit to doing the world a favor?' I suggested, and then felt a twinge of guilt for the comment. Just a twinge.

'Well, there is that.'

'How are the girls?' I asked, changing the subject.

'Asking more questions than I have answers to. But I think Bess and Alicia have finally figured out a way to keep Megan's mouth shut.'

'Duct tape?'

'Blackmail, I think. Every time she starts to say something about Graham, Bess turns to me and opens her mouth. Says, "Daaaad . . ." And then Megan looks panicked and runs from the room.'

'What do you think she did? Megan, I mean, that's blackmail-able.'

'God only knows with that girl,' he answered.

'You've checked that all the animals are OK?' I said. We have acquired quite a menagerie: two dogs, four cats, a gerbil, a turtle and somewhere between eight and twenty fish, depending on who's been found floating and been flushed.

'They seem OK.'

'Your wallet?'

'In my pocket. With a few bucks. As usual.'

'Well, keep an eye out for anything suspicious,' I said. 'Meanwhile, how's the Weaver job going?'

'Just some preliminary drawings and paperwork at this point. Won't really get started until sometime next week.'

'Are you going to have to hire some drafters?' I asked.

'Not right away, but maybe.'

I noticed Luna was stirring. I looked at the clock. It was

almost eight. 'Honey, I have to go. I think Luna might actually
be getting ready to call Champion.'

'When she's finished, check in with Stuart, OK? Unless
you've done that recently?'

'No, I haven't. And you're right. He needs to know about
our roofied theory.'

'Good luck,' he said. 'I love you.'

'You'd better,' I said with a smile. 'Back atja.'

'Afraid to say it in front of Luna?'

'Goodbye!' I said.

'Say it!' he said, laughing, while I hung up in his ear.

'I got nothin',' Champion said in answer to Luna's question.
'Gotta get a warrant to get the class rolls from last semester.
I'm going to see a judge this morning, but I wouldn't put my
hand over my ass waiting for it.'

'I rarely, if ever, put my hand over my ass,' Luna said.

'Sorry, just an expression.'

'No problem, I've heard it before. Listen, Nate, I'm thinking
there's a good chance the Pugh kid was roofied the night of
the murder. I questioned him and he admitted that when he
went to the cafeteria he left his food unattended for a moment
and fell asleep early – for him. Which might be why he never
woke up while all the killing was going on.'

'Hum,' Champion said. 'You actually got him to admit that
he might have been roofied?'

The sarcasm was not lost on Luna. 'Look, you should have
had him tested the next day but you didn't,' she said, letting
her voice get hard. 'It's probably too late now to find anything
in his system.'

'We can give it a shot. But I doubt if we'll find anything.'

'Only because it's Wednesday and he would have been
dosed Sunday night.'

'Or,' Champion said, his own voice going hard, 'he was
never dosed at all and was pretty much wide awake when
his roommate bought it. Or in a fugue state, as he's already
tried to imply.'

'*He* didn't imply that!' Luna said, anger building. 'I do
believe it was your girlfriend Gretchen Morley who said the

vic told her about the so-called middle of the night staring incidents.'

'Look, Luna, gotta go talk to the judge,' he said.

'Fine!' she said. 'But call me. Let me know what's going on.'

'I don't have to do that!' he said.

Luna sighed. 'I know you don't have to, Nate. And I'm sorry I got hostile. It's just this thing is hitting real close to home. I'd appreciate it if you'd keep me in the loop.'

'Yeah, whatever,' he said. Then, 'Maybe you can come with me to the admin building if I get the warrant. Then we can try to tackle that Fuchs guy, the student adviser.'

'*When* you get the warrant,' Luna said.

'Oh, yeah, positive thinking always works,' he said and hung up.

I called Stuart Freeman as soon as Luna got off the phone with Champion and headed into the bathroom for her shower. Mine would have to wait. Stuart himself picked up on the third ring.

'Law office,' he said.

'Stuart? It's E.J. Pugh.'

'Hey, E.J., what's up?'

'First, are congratulations in order for your assistant?' I asked.

'Yep. My first grandchild!' he said proudly.

'Oh, I didn't realize Maggie was your daughter.'

'Daughter-in-law. She came to work for me two years ago, my son came in, took one look and that's all she wrote folks!' he said with a laugh.

'And mom and baby?' I asked.

'Both great. A boy and they named him after me. Sort of. My middle name's Phillip. They named him Phillip Davis Freeman. Davis is Maggie's maiden name.'

'Well, that's certainly a name you can see on a ballot,' I said with a laugh.

'Or a judge's chamber door,' he said. 'Enough of that. You're calling for more than an update on Maggie, I'm betting.'

So I explained to him the theory Luna had come up with

– that Graham had been roofied, which was the reason he didn't wake up during the murder of his roommate.

'Hum,' he said. 'I like it. Heavy reasonable doubt. Any proof? Not that we need it for reasonable doubt, but I'm sure we'd both rather this never saw the inside of a courtroom.'

'Absolutely,' I said, beginning to perspire at the very thought of such a thing. 'We're hot on the trail of proof now.'

'You know, E.J., I need to tell you that you need to leave all this detective work to the police, right?'

I was quiet for a moment, listening in my head to the actual way he'd structured that sentence. Finally, I said, 'I know that you need to tell me that.'

'Then we're on the same page,' he said.

'OK.' I sighed. 'Congratulations on your new grandchild and please send Maggie my best wishes.'

'You got it. Keep me posted.'

'I will,' I said and hung up.

Graham made it to his seven a.m. class, and I got my shower, although between Graham in the next room and Luna in mine, the supply of hot water was zip to none. I knew Graham had another class at nine o'clock, with plans for a quick breakfast during the half-hour break. Then back-to-back classes until one-thirty. We'd planned for him to pick me up and go for lunch at that time. Meanwhile, my stomach was rumbling and I figured I needed sustenance to get me to that late lunch hour. I planned on having Luna drive me – and she could join me, no problem – to Threadgills, one of the older and better home-cookin' establishments in Austin, for breakfast. Unfortunately, or really fortunately for the case (for my stomach, not so much), Champion called her and wanted her to meet him at the U.T. admin building asap. Seems the judge he went to was an old Aggie alum and more than happy to sign papers to serve on his old rival. In Texas, these things can last a lifetime.

So I was on my own with no vehicle. I walked to the small lobby where I'd seen advertised a 'continental breakfast.' Checking it out, I discovered some limp fruit, frozen waffles and a bagel that had seen better days. The restaurant next to the hotel had a sign saying it was closed for plumbing repairs (and I really didn't even want to think about that!), so I checked my phone for other restaurants in the area. I finally found one only a couple of blocks from the motel. I'd only put on a sweater to walk to the motel lobby, so went back to my room to get my coat. In south central Texas, anything under sixty degrees is considered cold. It was fifty-five with no sun shining and the weatherman had said it could dip into the high forties. I cuddled up in my winter coat and headed out.

Unfortunately, the couple of blocks to the restaurant meant walking very, very carefully along the feeder road to IH 35, one of the more dangerous stretches of highway in the state. I walked in knee-high dead weeds along the side of the road until I found the place: a Mexican restaurant that served breakfast tacos. And, to my delight, they were delicious. That might have been more to do with the fact that I was ravenous than to the cooking skills of the kitchen help. But I ate two, bending my diet a bit, and found an alternative walk – through business driveways and yards – to the motel.

Where I waited for any word. From Luna, from Graham, from Willis. At that point I would have welcomed a phone call from a customer service rep. I even turned on the TV, and for someone with a loathing for daytime television, that's a good indicator of the tension and, let's face it, boredom I was enduring.

At shortly after one p.m., I was awakened by the honking of a horn outside my motel room. As I arose, I was surprised I could hear the honking above the noise of 'The Price is Right' blaring on the tube. I opened the door to find Graham and his beat-up Toyota awaiting me. I held up one finger to indicate I'd be a minute, then went in the bathroom and splashed water on my face. It didn't mess my makeup because in my rush to get to Austin I'd forgotten to pack any. But all I used it for mostly was to cover freckles, and my wintertime freckles weren't as obnoxious as those of other seasons.

I tried to hand-press the wrinkles out of the clothes I'd been sleeping in and headed out the door.

'What took you so long?' Graham asked, revving the aging engine then putting it in reverse and going entirely too fast backwards.

'Slow down!' I said.

He just shook his head. 'Where do you want to eat?' he asked.

'Threadgills!' was my immediate answer. Their breakfasts were legendary but their lunches and dinners were fairly epic as well.

The newer Threadgills – the one that hadn't been around in my college days – was much closer to the university, just over the river on the south side. The building had originally been a locally-owned cafeteria that catered mostly to the over-sixty crowd, but the conversion to the 'Keep Austin Weird' philosophy had been well done. Memorabilia from the old Armadillo World Headquarters adorned the place, like the piano Fats Domino played at a performance there, guitars signed by noted players, autographed pictures of all the blues, rock and roll and country stars who'd played there over the years. And of course, pictures of Janis Joplin playing with Kenneth Threadgill at the original Threadgills on Lamar, the one Willis and I would go to in our college days and bemoan the fact that we'd missed Janis by just a few years.

Even at one-thirty on a weekday afternoon, the place was crowded. Figuring being away from home meant calories didn't count, I ordered the chicken-fried steak, the San Antonio squash, the black-eyed pea salad and the yeast rolls. Graham had pretty much the same but went for the jalapeno cornbread. We were sitting there awaiting our orders, drinking large glasses of sweetened iced tea, when Graham said, 'Oh, crap, there's Gretchen Morley.' He nodded his head to the left and I looked.

'Who's that with her?' I asked, noting the small, teenaged Asian girl with her.

Graham shook his head. 'Don't know. But don't let her see us. She's the type to make a scene.' He turned to give the two a view of his back, but I wasn't quick enough. Gretchen Morley saw the two of us, got up and left the restaurant, leaving her companion behind.

'That was quick,' Luna said as she and Champion left the admin office earlier that morning. It had taken little more than an hour to show the warrant, be sent to the right department and for a coed working off a student loan to check her computer and come up with the two Brittanys who had been in that one-hundred-seat auditorium the semester before. One was surnamed Johnson and the other Barber.

'Aggie power at work,' Champion said with a smirk.

Luna just shook her head. 'At Texas Christian we were above such things,' she said.

'Bullshit,' was Champion's reply. Luna didn't argue the point.

'So which Brittany?' Luna asked. 'Did you get a description from Lexie Thurgood?'

He shook his head. 'Did you?'

She cut her eyes at him but refused to respond.

Finally, Champion said, 'I guess we could call her.'

'She's probably in class,' Luna said.

'Shit. So are both Brittanys, probably.'

'Well, let's at least find out where they both live,' Luna suggested.

'After we talk to that Fuchs guy,' Champion said.

'Oh, right! I keep forgetting about him,' Luna said. 'But I shouldn't. He's our most likely suspect so far.'

Champion gave her a look. 'Except, of course, for the Pugh kid.'

'Just don't,' Luna said, heading to the elevator.

Gaylord Fuchs' office was on the fourth floor and about as big as your standard broom closet. Crammed inside were a tiny desk and chair, two bookcases bulging with books and papers and magazines, and one visitors' chair.

They'd knocked on the door and been bidden to come in by a deep-throated voice. When they went in they found a man sitting tall in the chair behind the desk. He had dark brown hair receding at the hairline and a matching dark brown full beard. His eyebrows were dark and well groomed, and in such a perfect arch Champion wondered if they'd been plucked. He also had long black lashes over golden-brown eyes. He smiled when he saw them.

'I'm sorry, I thought you were students,' he said hopping down from what Champion now determined to be the adviser's very high stool.

The Pugh kid's comment that Fuchs looked like a ten-year-old was spot on: the man was maybe four foot two, with short legs and long arms. Champion wished the Pugh kid had mentioned the man was a little person. He held out his hand to Fuchs and said, 'Detective Champion, Austin PD, and this is Detective Luna, a consultant.'

'I thought y'all might be coming by. This is about Bishop Alexander, I presume?' Fuchs said.

'Yes. I understand you were his student adviser?' Champion asked.

'Yes, I was, and we were well into the second of the longest years of my life. Bishop Alexander was a pain in the ass.' He grinned. 'I thought I'd just get that out there right off the bat.' Spreading an arm toward the one visitors' chair, he said, 'Sit, please.' He walked around behind his desk and climbed up on his stool.

Champion indicated Luna take the chair while he remained standing. 'We understand you had an altercation with the young man?'

Fuchs made a hooting sound. 'Whoa! You could say that! I tried to beat the crap out of him but . . .' he indicated his body, '. . . I couldn't reach his face.'

'This was at a party—'

'At my house, yes,' Fuchs said. 'The asshole kept coming on to my wife and I ignored it for a while, and then he ran his hand up her skirt and pow, that was all she wrote!'

'Sounds like the kid was a real creep,' Luna said.

Fuchs was thoughtful for a moment, then said, 'Really, he was more than that. I'd say he was pathological about his need for attention. Especially from women. The other students who were at the party weren't that surprised about his behavior. I mean, a couple of them came up to tell me what he was doing. But my wife's a very independent woman; she doesn't need me coming to her rescue.'

'Yet you did,' Champion said.

Fuchs' cheeks turned a little red. 'Well, yeah, the Neanderthal came out in me that time. I mean, he touched her, for God's sake.'

'I can understand that,' Champion said. 'I've been married.

A person just doesn't do that, especially right in front of the husband.'

'Oh, yeah, it was a real "fuck you" to me. He wasn't getting the classes he wanted and I think this was his way of telling me off.'

'Did you ever visit Bishop in his dorm room?' Luna asked.

Fuchs shook his head. 'No, never.'

'So if we were to fingerprint you, we wouldn't find any matches in his room?'

'Maybe on some papers or pamphlets I've given him over the years, if he'd lowered himself to actually keep any, but other than that, no.' He held out his hands. 'You got the ink, I got the prints,' he said with a grin.

'You're not taking this very seriously, Mr Fuchs,' Luna said.

'Why would I? Personally, I hope you don't find whoever did this. But if you do, don't arrest them, just give 'em a medal. If anybody in this world needed killing, it was Bishop Alexander.'

'That's pretty harsh, Mr Fuchs,' Champion said.

'You know how many times that kid darkened my doorway? At least twice a week, sometimes three times a week. I've got one hundred and twelve kids I advise. I didn't have time for him but that didn't matter to that asshole. He'd actually push people out of the way to get into my office.' Fuchs sighed. 'So if you're looking at me as a suspect, I don't actually blame you, but I can give you the names of a bunch of kids he ran out of the office that might want to take a swing at him. And at that party, when he came on to my wife?'

'Yes?' Champion encouraged.

'Almost all the kids were bad-mouthing him big time, some really angry about other things he'd done. So, put me on your list, but it'll have to be as long as a roll of toilet paper to handle all the names.'

Luna stood up. 'Thanks for your time, Mr Fuchs. And for your candor.'

Fuchs hopped down from his stool and held out his hand to shake those of both detectives. 'If y'all need anything else, holler,' he said and handed Champion a business card. 'My home number's on the back,' he said. 'I let all my kids have one.' He sighed. 'Which was a big mistake when it came to Bishop.'

After leaving Fuchs' office, they went back to the clerk who had sent them to Records. She sighed long and hard but came up with addresses of the two Brittanys. One lived off-campus and the other lived in the B&B. Since the dorm was closest, they headed that way. The coed in the office of the dorm reacted swiftly to Champion's badge and gave them the room number for Brittany Johnson. There was no answer to their knock on her door, so Champion took out a business card, wrote *Please call this number asap* on the back and stuck it between the door and the jamb, then they headed to the off-campus home of Brittany Number Two.

Brittany Barber lived in a post-war bungalow about five miles from campus. There were three cars in the driveway and a rack in the front yard for about six bicycles, three of which were in residence. Luna figured by its size it couldn't have had more than two bedrooms. There was no bell for the door so Champion knocked rather hard.

The door was almost immediately flung open and a young white man with dreadlocks stood staring out at them. He had a backpack over his shoulder and a shocked look on his face. Then he grinned and said, 'Man, you scared the shit out of me! I was just about to head out and, wham! You hit the door! Who do you want?'

'Brittany Barber,' Champion said.

The boy frowned. 'You're not her dad. Why do you want her?'

Champion again showed his badge. 'We need to ask her a few questions,' he said.

Over his shoulder, the young man yelled, 'Brit! The cops!' Turning to Champion, he said, 'Man, I gotta boogy or I'm gonna miss my class.' He pushed past them and headed down the porch to the bike rack, grabbed one of the bikes, jumped on and headed down the street, leaving the door open behind him.

Champion and Luna moved into what should have been a living room. Instead it was furnished with two mattresses on the floor and a couple of beat-up easy chairs. A young woman came out of the next room – which ordinarily Luna would have thought was used as a dining room, but in this instance, that room, too, contained mattresses but no easy chairs. There were boxes littering the floor with peoples' names on them.

'Hey,' the young woman said, coming into the erstwhile living room. She was of medium height and medium build, with dark brown hair reaching past her waist. She wore no makeup but didn't really need to. The peaches-and-cream complexion on its own highlighted the bright green eyes. 'I'm Brittany. You're the cops?'

'Yes, ma'am. I just need to ask you a few questions,' Champion said.

The girl threw up her hands, grinned real big and said, 'I swear I didn't do it!'

Champion's return smile was tight. 'You were in Professor Winston's economics class last semester, is that correct?'

The smile left her face as she lowered her arms and tilted her head to the side. 'Yeah.'

'Did you know a young woman named Lexie Thurgood?'

A frown developed. 'Yeah. Is she OK?'

'Yes, ma'am,' Champion said. 'There were two Brittanys in that class and we're just trying to locate the one who told Miss Thurgood something.'

Again the tilt of the head. 'OK. What?'

'About overhearing something Bishop Alexander may have said.'

The young woman sank down on one of the mattresses in the living room. 'Oh, shit! This is about that murder at the McMillan, right?'

'Yes, ma'am,' Champion said. 'Did you mention something to Miss Thurgood about overhearing a slur uttered by Mr Alexander?'

'Well, yeah. It was right before winter break. I was hanging out in the quad and this guy Bobby somebody was sitting there with what were *obviously* his parents, and that asshole Bish – sorry, I shouldn't speak ill of the dead and all that, but, God, he *was* an asshole. I mean, look up the word in *Webster's* and man, like there's his picture, you know?'

'Do you remember what he said?' Champion asked.

The girl appeared to think for a moment, then said, 'Well,

it was to the effect that he, Bishop, had been waiting for him
and who the fuck – his word – did he think he was keeping
him, Bishop, waiting? I mean, he was almost screaming it,
and then the kid says, like "Hey, man, these are my folks,"
and Bishop goes, "Who the fuck cares? *You* don't keep *me*
waiting *ever!* You understand me, you piece of shit?" By this
time both the kid's parents were standing up and the mother's
hands were, like, you know, fists, and I thought for a minute
she was going to clock him, but then Bishop goes, "Whatever!"
And just walks away.'

'Did you hear what the parents said to the kid?' Luna asked,
for a second forgetting that this was supposed to be Champion's
show.

'Yeah, like his father goes, "Who was that?" And his mother
goes, "Who the hell does he think he is?" And then the kid
just pats their shoulders, going, "He was just kidding. He
kids!"' She shook her head. 'Can you believe that shit? I mean,
man, if somebody ever, I mean *ever* talked to me like that – in
front of my folks or not – I'd . . .' She stopped for a minute
then said, 'I was about to say I'd kill 'em.' She shrugged.
'Maybe that's what happened?' she asked, cocking her head.

'Thank you for your time, Miss Barber,' Champion said.

She stood up from the mattress on the floor. 'Sure, no
problem. But, Detective, for future reference?'

'Yes, ma'am?'

'It's Ms not miss, OK?' She smiled as she walked them to
the door and shut it behind them.

'No more classes?' I asked my son.

'Not until tomorrow.'

'So how was the seven a.m.?'

'Early,' he said.

'I mean as a class,' I said.

He shrugged. 'Got way too much to read. Missing the first
day may have screwed me up.'

'So we go back to the motel and you read,' I suggested.

As he was driving, he looked my way for just a second then
back at the road. 'I'd rather be finding out who the asshole
was that dosed me and killed my roommate.'

'That won't help you pass the class,' I said.

'Mom, just don't, OK? Just don't.'

'Don't what?'

'Do that – that *mom* shit!'

'How can I not do the, excuse the expression, *mom* shit? I'm your mom.'

'I don't need Mom right now,' my son, the ungrateful little creep, said. 'I need E.J. Pugh, the woman who finds out who did what. That's who I need!'

'I'm here,' I said quietly. 'I am E.J. Pugh, the woman who finds out who did what, but I'm also your mother.' I sighed. 'Let's compromise. You go to your room and read until Luna gets back. Then we all get together and decide where to go next.'

He made a 'harrumphing' sound, then said, 'If she'll even talk to us. Seems she just wants to hang out with that asshole detective. Maybe she's helping him find more shit to charge me with!'

'You know that's not true,' I said, wishing and hoping my words were correct.

'I don't know squat,' he said, leaning forward against the steering wheel, his shoulders hunched. 'Let's just get back to the motel. Then whatever.'

We pulled into the parking spot in front of Graham's motel room. The spot in front of my room was occupied by Luna's car. With the engine still running, Graham asked, 'Did she take her car or did Champion pick her up?'

'Her car wasn't here when you picked me up,' I said.

'Yeah, you're right.' He turned the key to the off position and we heard the Toyota's engine spurt and sputter for a few minutes before it finally died.

'Shall we go in?' I asked him.

He sighed. 'Yeah. Can't dance. There's no music.'

I left that line alone and used my key to let us in the motel room. Luna was propped against the headboard of her bed, several pillows behind her back, the TV remote in her hand, flicking through the channels. On seeing us, she said, 'Boy, there's a lot of crap on daytime TV.'

'True,' I said, throwing my purse on my bed and hopping on, imitating her position against the headboard.

'So this is what you do?' Graham asked, arms akimbo. 'Sit on your asses and watch TV while I'm being harassed by the cops and probably headed for the gas chamber?'

Luna flicked to another channel. 'We don't use gas chambers any more,' she said. 'It's the needle.'

'Thank you, Lieutenant Luna,' my son said with a bite of sarcasm I was proud to say came from my genes. 'I feel all warm and fuzzy inside.'

'Glad to help,' Luna said, trying another channel. 'Don't they have pay-per-view movies or anything?'

'Goddammit!' Graham shouted.

Luna and I both looked up from the TV. 'Graham!' I said sternly.

'*Mother!*' he said just as sternly back.

I sighed. 'Luna, turn off the TV.'

She kept scrolling channels.

'Please,' I said.

'I was just waiting for the "P" word,' she said as she turned off the TV. 'Now say thank you.'

'Thank you,' I parroted. 'Now, what did you and Champion find out?'

'Well, we met with Bishop's student adviser, Gaylord Fuchs.' Turning to Graham, she said, 'You could have mentioned he was a little person.'

Graham raised his eyebrows. 'Oh, that explains why he's so short!'

'Jesus, Pugh,' Luna said to me, 'have you taught this kid nothing?'

I shrugged. 'I'll admit he's not terribly observant, but then what twenty-year-old is?'

Luna sighed. 'He was very open about his dislike of Bishop,' she said. 'And yes, your roommate did come onto the guy's wife and the guy did try to punch him out but missed. He basically said he might be on the list of those who wanted to kill Bishop but that the list was very, very long.'

'He's got that right,' Graham said, sinking down on the bed next to me. 'I think you've met the only two people in the world who liked him. Gretchen and Bobby.'

'What about other girlfriends?' Luna asked.

Graham shrugged. 'No actual girlfriends,' he said. 'He'd date a girl until he got in her pants—' He looked quickly at me and said, 'Sorry, Mom. Anyway, after that he'd drop them. So I doubt any of them had a great love for the asshole.'

'So this Fuchs guy,' I said. 'Does he seem viable?'

'As viable as anybody else on campus,' Luna said.

'But more viable than me, right?' Graham said, a pleading note to his voice.

'We need to prove you were roofied,' Luna said. 'The big problem is the fact that you were in the room when he got killed.'

'How do we prove that?' I asked.

Luna shook her head. 'Since Graham's blood wasn't tested that morning, we can't. The only way is to find out who *did* kill the little darlin' and doped Graham.'

'What about that girl Lexie told you about?' Graham said.

'We found the girl who told Lexie about Bishop's behavior with Bobby and his folks.' She looked at Graham. 'How could you stand this guy?'

He sank down on the bed next to me. 'I couldn't. That's part of the problem! He was such an asshole everybody thinks I musta done it and don't really blame me. Except Champion, I guess. Pretty sure he blames me.'

'Well, we're looking at Bobby Dunston's parents. They were pretty upset with what Bishop said, according to this girl who overheard it.'

'What's her name?' Graham asked. 'The girl.'

'Brittany Barber.'

Graham shook his head. 'Don't know her.'

'Big campus,' Luna said.

'Yeah,' he conceded. He sighed. 'So what do we do now?'

'I'd like a little more quality time with Gretchen Morley,' Luna said. 'I like her a lot.' Turning to look at us, she said, 'Not as a person, as a suspect.'

'Good,' Graham said. 'I'd have to re-think everything I know about you if you liked that bitch as a person.'

'Graham, you really should watch your mouth,' I said to my son.

'Go away, Mom. We need E.J.'

Luna looked from one to the other of us. 'Huh?' she said.

'Inside joke, sort of,' I said. Then, remembering, I told her, 'We saw Gretchen at Threadgills around one-thirty today. She took one look at us and hightailed it out of there.'

'Guilty conscience?' Luna said.

'Could be,' I answered.

'So let's go talk to her again!' Graham said, getting up from the bed. 'If she's scared of us let's keep it up! Maybe she'll do something that'll help us prove she did it!'

Luna didn't move from her reclining position. 'Did you see Gretchen in the cafeteria Sunday night?' she asked.

'No, but there were a lot of—'

'People, yeah, you said that. But wouldn't you have noticed if Bishop's ex-girlfriend was there?'

'I don't know!' he said, sinking back down on the bed. 'I mean, I wasn't looking for anybody. Sorta kept my head down and just grabbed some food.'

'And we need to talk about your choice of dinner—' I started, but he interrupted.

'Go *away*, Mom!'

'So what new questions do you have for Morley?' Luna asked.

Graham thought for a moment. 'You told her there was a witness to her keying the car—'

'Yeah, but I lied,' Luna said.

'Yeah, I know. But you could lie again. Say a witness has come forward who saw her dose me! Yeah! That'd be good! Say that!'

'And what if she is involved in some way with Bishop's death – like she stabbed him,' I said, 'but somebody else roofied you. Luna says there's a witness to something she knows she didn't do and she knows we're lying. The jig, as they say, is up.'

'Nobody says that,' my son said, his voice sulky. 'So have *you* got any bright ideas?' he asked, staring at me in a not particularly friendly way.

'Follow-up questions for Gretchen Morley,' I said, grabbing my pad of paper and a pen from the bedside table. 'Number one?' I turned expectantly toward Luna.

She shrugged her shoulders. 'Not my idea.'

'Well, it may not be your idea but you're the professional. Surely you have something to say to this young woman?' I prompted.

'You mean other than "Get a life? Lighten up, bitch? Stop the hysterics and answer some serious questions"?'

Graham and I both sat up on the bed. 'Yeah, that!' he said, pointing at Luna.

'Exactly,' I said.

'Fine,' she said. 'But what are the serious questions?'

'I don't know—' Graham started with a little heat in his voice but stopped when his phone rang. He looked at the screen. 'It's a Houston area code,' he said, looking at me.

'Who do you know in Houston? Other than your grandparents,' I amended.

'Their names would come up, not the number.' He looked from me to Luna. 'Think it could be Bishop's mom?'

'Why would she be calling you?' I asked.

'Just answer the goddam phone!' Luna shouted.

'Oh, right!' Graham said, answering it on speaker. 'Hello?'

'Graham?' It was a woman's voice.

'Yes?' he said, looking from me to Luna and back again.

'This is Adrianne Alexander, Bishop's mother,' the voice said.

'Oh, hey, Mrs Alexander,' Graham said. 'I'm real sorry about—'

'Yes, yes, of course,' she said, interrupting. 'I'm on my way to Austin now. Just going through LaGrange as we speak. I need to meet with you as soon as I get there.'

'Sure, ma'am. Ah, you want me to meet you some place?'

'I assume you're not in the dorm room you shared with my son,' she said. It wasn't a question.

'No, ma'am—'

'Where are you staying?' she asked.

'At a motel on IH 35. The Island Paradise.'

'What room?' she asked.

He gave her the room number.

'I'll be there in less than an hour. Don't leave.' And with that, she hung up.

I shook my head at the complete lack of emotion in the woman's voice. I know people grieve differently but her demeanor had been almost friendly. Surely *that's* not normal? 'Can't wait to meet this broad!' I said.

'You're going to have to,' Luna said. 'I don't want her to know that Graham's not alone. We're going to stay in here with your cell phone open on speaker, connected to Graham's cell phone on speaker—'

'She'll see it!' Graham said.

Luna sighed. 'Put it slightly under one pillow. Make sure she sits on the bed where you put it. And if she asks you if you're alone, say you called your folks but they're in Europe right now, trying to get home. Got it?'

'Yeah. You want me to lie to a woman who just lost her son?' Graham said.

'Yes, Graham, I want you to lie. By the sound of her voice on the phone, I'd say the woman has an agenda and you're part of it. Let's see what she has to say.'

Graham shrugged. 'Whatever.'

I looked at my son, taking his hands in mine. 'Honey, I know you can do it. You're an excellent liar.'

'Mom!'

'Mom's gone, remember?'

'Jeez,' my son said.

'And you can get in some of that reading for the seven a.m. class while you're waiting.'

NINE

'Do I call Champion and tell him the vic's mom is on her way?' Luna said, I thought more to herself than to me. I didn't answer. She turned abruptly and stared at me. 'Well?' she demanded.

'Oh, sorry! I thought it was a rhetorical question,' I said.

'I don't do rhetorical,' she said.

'So you want *my* opinion on whether or not you should call Champion? I thought my answer would be obvious.'

'Yeah, you're right. You vote for no. I'm sure Graham votes for no—'

I grinned and spread out my hands. 'Majority rule!' I said.

'Not in a police investigation,' she said.

'Yes, but you're not in your jurisdiction. So you're not really police here, right?'

'Right.' She turned and looked at me. 'It would be just as easy to tell Champion what we overhear after we overhear it,' she said.

'Right,' I agreed. 'And he'd probably frown on us listening in to her conversation with Graham.'

'Say something stupid like entrapment. Which it isn't!' she said.

'Absolutely not!' I agreed again, frowning. 'No such thing!'

Luna sighed. 'So we wait. If what she has to say to Graham is nothing then we just let Champion know she's in town and leave it at that. But if she's got something interesting to say—'

'We record it!' I said, holding up my phone.

'That will record a conversation?'

'Yep,' I said.

'You know that's against the law—'

'For the police. Not for private citizens.'

She sighed again. 'I've never been good at walking a tight-rope,' she said.

'I'll hold your hand,' I assured her, and got a glare for my kind words.

We heard a car pull up and Luna moved to the window, peering through a crack in the blinds. 'Beamer with a faux blonde inside,' she said.

'Probably her,' I said and rang Graham's cell. To him, I said, 'I think she just drove up. Stick the phone under the pillow!'

'Gotja!' he said, and I could hear the rustle of the bed-clothes as he tucked the phone away. Then, quite clearly, through the wall and the phone, we heard a rap on Graham's door.

He opened the door and said, 'Mrs Alexander?'

'*Ms* Alexander,' she said. She must have pushed past him because all of a sudden her voice was closer to the phone.

'Please, ma'am, have a seat.' There was another, slighter rustle of the bedclothes.

'I need to talk to you,' the woman said.

'Yes, ma'am.'

'Did you get a chance to grab any of Bishop's things?'

'Ah, no, ma'am. I didn't even get a chance to grab my thing—'

'So the police have already searched the room,' she said. Again, not a question.

'Yes, ma'am,' Graham answered anyway.

'When can you get back in?' she asked.

'I don't know. Maybe never. Ma'am, I need to tell you that the police consider me a suspect.'

She was quiet for a moment, then asked, very matter-of-factly, 'Did you kill my son?'

'No, ma'am,' Graham said.

'Good. OK,' she said, and we could tell she'd stood up by the creak of the bed springs and the fact that her voice seemed slightly farther away. 'Please don't tell anyone I was here,' she said.

'Ma'am,' Graham said, and we could tell he too was standing. 'I'm not sure what it was you wanted to see me about.'

Ms Alexander was quiet for a moment, then said, 'I think Bishop may have had something of mine. I would like to get it back before the police take it for some reason.'

'Oh,' Graham said, 'I see,' which he clearly didn't.

'Thank you for your time,' she said as her voice dimmed the nearer she got to the door.

'If there's anything else—' Graham started but she interrupted him.

'No, of course not. Why would there be?' And seconds later we heard her Beamer start up.

Luna and I looked at each other. 'Whoa. What a piece of work!' Luna said.

I picked up the phone and said, 'Graham?'

'Yeah?' he said.

'Aren't you glad I'm your mother?'

There was a beat before he said, 'Actually, yeah, I think I am.'

'You did what?' Champion shouted into the phone.

'She was only here for a few seconds—' Luna started.

'Not the effing point, Luna! Jeez! You should have called me the minute she contacted the kid! Jesus H! What were you thinking?' he stormed on.

'If you'd rather yell at me then find out what she asked Graham—'

'Goddammit, Luna!' He sighed heavily over the phone line. 'What did she want?'

'She thought the vic may have had something of hers. She wanted in the dorm room was the impression I got. She was hoping Graham could get her in. Probably the only reason she spoke to him. She didn't seem that concerned about her son's death.'

'Obviously not if she was talking to the Pugh kid!' he said.

'So I'm thinking—'

'Don't!' he said. 'Don't think. When you think I get in trouble! So stop!'

'What if,' Luna went on, oblivious to what he said, 'we have Graham call her back? Her number's in his cell phone. He tells her that he has a way to get into the dorm room. And maybe he can help her . . .'

'You're treading on entrapment here,' he said.

Still ignoring him, she went on: 'Find whatever it is she wants. All she has to do is describe it—'

'And if it's something incriminating you think she'd do that? "Here, kid, go find the murder weapon for me then come stand here while I stab you so there'll be no witnesses."'

'Or she goes with him—'

'Entrapment!'

'Not necessarily! If you're in the room waiting for her, yeah. But what if you're outside the door, just on your way in to check for something—'

'What?'

'I don't know!' Luna said, getting frustrated. 'You can think of something to help, can't you? Anyway, she walks out with the Pugh kid and something in her hand, and you, of course, can't let her take anything out of the room as yet—'

'So then I arrest both her and the kid. Not bad,' he said.

'You don't have to do that,' Luna said, back-peddling. 'Just confiscate whatever she took and give them both a stern talking to.'

'I'd really like to get that kid behind bars,' he said.

'If he's helping you with the investigation? I know his mother well. She'll sue your ass.'

He sighed. 'Yeah, and there would go the dollar and a half I have left from the divorce.'

'You wouldn't want to lose that,' Luna said, a smile in her voice.

'Yeah, I wanna keep it to buy a lottery ticket.'

'You never know,' she said.

He sighed again. 'Unfortunately, I do.'

'OK, so she was a piece of work,' I said to Luna, 'but do you really think she killed her own son?'

'I just want to know what's so important that she needs to get into his dorm room to confiscate it before the police do,' she said.

'You think he took something that could incriminate her in some dastardly deed so she killed him to hush it up?' I postulated.

'And didn't look for it while she was in there stabbing her son? With the knowledge that his roommate was out cold?' She shook her head, reversing her position. It was something the two of us tended to do. 'She would have searched thoroughly if that were the case.'

'I don't know,' I continued, 'it has to be bad on the psyche to kill your own child, so maybe she panicked and just ran.'

'So you think it would be traumatic to kill your child?'

'Well, duh.'

She leaned back on the pillows of her bed. 'Not buying it. There's something there, I grant you. But I just don't think she killed her kid.'

'Why? Because she's so warm and loving?' I said. OK, a little sarcastically.

'What's your problem with this woman?' she asked.

'You mean besides the fact that she was a rotten mother who raised a rotten son and didn't seem to give a shit about him? Other than that, she seems like a peach of a gal.'

'Rotten mothers don't necessarily kill their children. If they did, we wouldn't have so many rotten kids. And besides, some people manage to raise themselves up from abusive beginnings.'

Having just remembered that Eduardo, her husband, had been raised in an abusive household, I decided to shut my mouth. The fact that he'd spent twenty years in Leavenworth for killing his commanding officer – in self-defence – was an argument against what she'd just said, but I thought it best, under the circumstances, to let it go.

'So what did Champion say?' I asked instead. 'Is he going to do it?'

She shrugged. 'He didn't say no,' she said. 'He didn't say yes either but he didn't say no.'

'And that's significant?'

'I believe so,' she said with a hint of a smirk. 'Let's go talk to Graham, just in case.'

So we went to his room, knocking on the door, only to have it opened by a pretty young woman with lots of curly brown hair and big brown eyes. She smiled big and held out her hand to me. 'You must be Graham's mom,' she said. 'He looks just like you!'

'I am,' I said, smiling back. 'And you are?'

'Miranda Wisher. You know, the girl who left the evidence in your son's room?'

The smile seemed glued to my face. She was certainly upfront about it. Maybe a little too upfront? Oh, yeah. A lot too upfront. On my list of things I didn't want to know, that would be number one. So what was I supposed to say? *Nice to meet you?* Or, *You did a good job cleaning up the mess?* Or simply, *Go away before I start to scream!*

Luna saved the situation by moving past me into the motel room. 'You need to make a statement to the detective in charge,' she said to the girl in passing. Then turned to my son, who was on one of the beds on his stomach, a book in front of him.

'Miranda's helping me with tomorrow's government assignment. She's in the same class. The one I missed on Tuesday.'

'That's nice,' I said, finally finding my tongue.

'Can we talk about the problem in front of her?' Luna said, never one to beat about the bush.

'Oh, yeah, she knows everything I know,' Graham said, smiling at the girl. I mean, young woman.

'And anyone who thinks Graham could have hurt a fly, much less kill that obnoxious prick, Bishop, is out of their freaking mind,' she said, sitting down entirely too close to my son.

Lighten up, I tried to tell myself. It's not like they haven't already done it. I had more or less doubted my twenty-year-old son was still a virgin, but having this evidence of it made me sad.

'Well, your mom and I came up with an idea and I've put it before Champion. Now we have to wait and see what his decision is,' Luna said.

Graham frowned, looking back and forth between Luna and myself. 'Do I want to know?'

'You're instrumental to the plan,' I said, 'so yeah, you want to know.'

'Are you going to get me killed or arrested?' he asked.

'Neither,' Luna said. Then, to everyone's chagrin, added: 'I hope.'

Miranda Wisher's head was swiveling from one speaker to the next, like a member of the audience at a tennis match. 'Wait, now!' she said. 'Isn't he already in enough trouble? What are y'all talking about?'

'Does she really need to be here?' Luna asked Graham.

'Yes!' Miranda said. Graham grinned at her, then said to Luna, 'I doubt I could get rid of her if I wanted to.'

'You got that right, buster!' the girl said.

'So what is it you want me to do that might get me killed or arrested?' Graham asked.

We laid out the plan we'd presented to Champion shortly before.

'Hum,' Graham said. 'I don't see how I could get killed *or* arrested for that.'

'If she killed her son, she might kill you, too,' Luna offered.

'Yeah, I guess there *is* that,' Graham agreed. 'But do you think she did?'

Luna used her head to point at me. 'Your mother does,' she said.

'That's only because she's thought about killing all her kids at one time or another,' Graham said, grinning at me.

'It's been a while,' I admitted, 'but don't push me.'

'So why would I get arrested?' he asked.

'I doubt you will. If Champion agrees to this, you won't.'

'What are the chances he's going to agree?' Graham asked.

Luna shrugged. 'Fifty-fifty? No, probably more like sixty-forty. Or less.'

'So what do we do if he says no?' Graham asked.

Luna and I looked at each other. 'We go to plan B,' I said.

'Which is?' Graham asked.

I shrugged, and Luna said, 'We'll work on that if we need to.'

Nate Champion was thinking hard. He'd searched the vic's room himself and found nothing that could incriminate the mother. To his knowledge, he had to admit. What if there had been something there that he didn't recognize as incriminating? But asking the Pugh kid to get involved in setting up the vic's mother was a stretch and a half, as far as he was concerned. Of course, the vic's mother had been the one to approach the kid, so that *would* be just about the only way to do it.

He sighed and looked at the phone on his desk. He could just call Luna and get the ball rolling but he was still hesitant.

Luna had been right about one thing: he hadn't had the Pugh
kid's blood tested the morning the body was discovered. He
probably should have done that. If the kid had been roofied,
as the three of them claimed, then the chances were good he
didn't do it. And, other than the fact that his roommate was
an asshole and he disliked him intensely, why else would the
kid do it? Champion himself had had an asshole for a roommate his freshman year at A&M – Gordo Bacon. Gordo
thought flushing heads was an Olympic sport. But Champion
hadn't killed him. He could admit, if only to himself, that he'd
thought about it the third time his head had been shoved
in the toilet, but he hadn't done it. And as far as witnesses
went, no one had ever seen Bishop Alexander get physical
with the Pugh kid.

'So what are you saying?' he asked himself. 'You no longer
think the Pugh kid is your top suspect?' He studied that thought.
Had he taken the kid off his list? If so, who was left? The
Morley girl, the one he thought of in his head as Pretty Poison.
The Thurgood girl? He shook his head. She just didn't seem
the type. Maybe he should look at her further, but he wasn't
sure why.

Then there was the mother. The vic's mother. Luna had told
him what the Pugh kid had said about his knowledge of her
relationship with her son – if he wasn't lying. 'Get off his
case!' he said to himself. 'For just a minute. You can always
go back.' Taking his own advice, he delved more into the
mother. The only relationship with the mother prior to the
kid's death seemed to be a financial one. She sent him money,
he spent it and asked for more. Did she give it to him? Was
that what she was looking for? Was she strapped and needed
cash? But by what the Pugh kid had said, the vic spent every
dime just as quick as he could. Surely, if he kept calling home
for more, his mother would have to know that the likelihood
of there being any spare cash lying around Bishop's things
was nil. So what was she looking for?

Sunday night had been the first night back in the dorms after
winter break. So, had Bishop gone home over the break? Had
he been with his mother? Had he seen something, heard something? Or merely taken something? From what he'd heard

about this kid, he wouldn't have any scruples about stealing, especially from his own mother.

Champion sighed long and hard and picked up the phone, hitting the redial for Luna's cell phone.

'So here's the deal,' Champion said to Graham. 'You meet her in the lobby of McMillan Hall, you take her up the stairs—'

'Hey, that's four floors!' Graham complained.

'It'll make it look more like you're sneaking in,' Champion said.

'But she's old, so—' Graham started.

'Your mom and I saw her from the window,' Luna said. 'She looked like a gymoholic to me.'

'Very fit,' I concurred.

'Shit,' Graham said under his breath.

'Are we doing this or what?' Champion demanded.

'Yeah, yeah, we're doing it,' Graham said grudgingly.

'So, OK. You take the stairs to your room. There will be a seal on the door. You can break it with a pocket knife or even a fingernail. You got a pocket knife?' he asked.

'Yes, I have a pocket knife,' Graham said between clenched teeth.

'Honey, if you don't want to do this—' I started but was interrupted.

'No, no. It may be the only way to clear my name,' he said, his eyes shooting daggers in Champion's direction.

'You got that right,' Champion agreed. 'So you break the seal, and this is important: no matter what she says, you go in with her, got that?'

'Yes.'

'And what does he do once he's in there?' I asked.

'He stands around and watches her. Covertly, of course,' Luna said.

'Then if she does find something and goes to leave, you make sure you see where she puts it. Whatever it is,' Champion said. 'It can't be too big or I would have found it. Chances are she'll stick it in a pocket or her purse or something. When you come out and see me, try to let me know where she put it. Got that?'

'What? Point? Say "There it is"?'

'Try using your eyeballs!' Champion suggested. 'Or your head. Try, if you can possibly do it, to be discreet.'

'Whatever,' Graham said.

I was beginning to have misgivings about this whole caper. How close to the legal definition of entrapment was this? What if she didn't find anything? What if Graham didn't see where she put it? Were they going to strip-search her? That would be a job and a half.

'Where's your phone?' Champion asked. Graham held it up. 'Make the call,' he said.

Graham found the number from which the Alexander woman had called and looked at me. I nodded and he hit redial, putting the phone on speaker.

'Yes?' came the woman's disembodied voice.

'Ms Alexander, this is Graham Pugh, Bishop's room—'

'I know who you are,' she said.

'Well, I've been thinking about what you asked and I think I have a way of getting into my dorm room.'

'Good,' she said. 'I'm at the Four Seasons. It shouldn't take you more than fifteen minutes to get here.' She gave him her room number, told him to come up the service elevator and hung up.

'I'm beginning to feel sorry for Bishop,' Graham said.

'I'm just delighted the comparisons are so much in my favor,' I said.

'Don't think this'll last forever, Mom,' Graham said, rising from his bed. 'So, I'll take my car?'

TEN

Champion tried to get rid of the Pugh woman. 'You stay here—' he started, shortly after her son had driven off in his car.

She laughed. 'Not on your life!'

'Ma'am, this is a police investigation—'

'Forget it, Nate,' Luna said. 'It doesn't work. If we don't take her with us she'll find some way of getting there on her own.' She sighed and shrugged her shoulders. 'That's just the way she is. And it's better to have her with us rather than running around on her own mucking things up.'

The mom glared at Luna. 'I don't muck things up! But other than that, you've got it right!' the mom had declared. 'So?'

Champion had just given his head a shake and walked out the door to his unmarked car, the two women trailing behind. At least she sat in the back seat, he told himself, which meant she'd have to have someone open the door for her. He grinned, thinking to himself how he could just leave her there. Then the scenario of her screaming her head off in front of McMillan Hall and every student in a five-mile radius running up to see what the drama was came to his mind and he figured letting her out of the back seat might be the best bet.

Graham had no idea how to find the service elevator at the Four Seasons. He thought if he asked that would just draw attention. He supposed the whole reason Bishop's mom wanted him to come up the service elevator was to avoid drawing attention. Or she thought of him as a lesser being who didn't deserve the finery of the hotel's main elevator. Probably both, he decided. He then opted for the main elevator. It was nice and he managed not to dirty it with his unworthy germs, he thought to himself. He found her room without a problem and knocked on the door.

Adrianne Alexander opened it, looked at Graham and turned

her back, leaving the door open. Graham came in the room and shut the door behind him, then noticed it wasn't exactly a room – it was a suite. And a nice one, too. He wondered if maybe he and his mom could move into the Four Seasons for the duration of this mess. Then thought that the cost might come out of his senior year tuition.

'We'll take my car,' the woman said.

'OK.'

'Well?' she declared.

'Ah . . . Oh, you wanna go now?'

'Would you rather I call room service for cocktails and appetizers?'

Having been raised by E.J. Pugh, Graham knew sarcasm when he heard it. 'Ah, I couldn't find the service elevator—' he started.

She sighed. 'Whatever. Take the elevator to the garage level and wait near the doors. Not in front of them but near them. Do you understand?'

'Yes, ma'am,' Graham said.

'Then go!'

'Ah, yes, ma'am,' Graham said, biting his tongue. On the way down in the elevator he thought of all those things he could have said to Bishop now that he himself had spent some quality time with Bishop's mother. Things like, 'I know a good therapist.'

He did as he was told, stood off to the side of the elevator doors and waited for his roommate's mother to show up. She took her time. By his watch, he'd stood there for over five minutes before she came out of the elevator. When she did, she totally ignored him and headed to her car. Graham followed behind – at a discreet distance. She got into her Beamer, unlocking the passenger side with her key fob and then started the car. Graham hurried into the passenger seat.

The woman left rubber as she screeched out of the parking lot, so fast Graham felt the need to hold on to the handle by the door. She didn't look as she came out of the exit, and Graham saw a car screeching to a halt and another running up on the sidewalk to avoid her. Ms Alexander didn't seem to notice.

It was early evening and the sidewalk in front of McMillan Hall was crowded with students rushing somewhere, anywhere. Others were just standing around, talking in small groups, sitting on steps with a book on their laps or just staring off into space, depending on whether the evening's refreshments had already been imbibed or inhaled. Ms Alexander dropped Graham off in front of the McMillan dorm and headed to find a parking space, leaving Graham terse instructions to hide in the stairwell until she found him. He did as he was told, apologizing to Bishop in his mind. The stairwell stunk. It was a mixture of urine and vomit, the traditional smells of a dorm that housed a lot of freshmen.

It took twice as long for her to find him in the stairwell as it had for her to show up in the parking garage at the hotel. When she finally did, she didn't say a word, just began walking up the stairs at a brisk pace. Graham hadn't even had to suggest they use the stairs – she'd come up with the same idea on her own. So, Graham considered, she really was up to no good. He thought he might be getting out of this predicament sooner than he'd anticipated.

Once on the fourth floor, she used her head to indicate that he go first through the door that led to the corridor. He opened it gingerly, checking right and left. There was no one in the hall. He motioned her forward but she refused. 'You go open the room door. I'll come in after you,' she said.

Graham sighed, nodded and headed out into the hall.

I was beginning not to like Nate Champion very much. I'd earlier thought he was nice to look at but familiarity not only breeds contempt, it also strips one of any allure. I was beginning to see the hairs in his ears and the wrinkles in his neck – whether they were there or not. I do have my fickle side. He had stuck me in the back seat of his unmarked car. Although it was unmarked, it still had those lovely police vehicle amenities of no door handles on the back doors. I knew I was only a whim away from being stuck in the car while Luna and Champion dealt with whatever was going to transpire.

I thought reminding Champion of how helpful I'd been and

could continue to be might help my situation. 'So did we tell you about seeing Gretchen Morley at Threadgills?' I asked.

'No,' he said.

'Ah, yeah, well, we did. Graham and I. She was sitting there with another girl, but when she saw us she got up and left.'

'No doubt thinking she didn't want to eat in the same room as the guy who killed the love of her life,' the asshole said.

'Jeez, Nate, give it a break,' Luna said, obviously reading my mind.

'Or she was feeling guilty and thought we were watching her!' I countered.

'Or she was through eating and left,' he said.

'She just left her friend sitting there all by herself. And her plate looked like she hadn't finished it—'

'Grief will take away your appetite,' he said.

'Why are you being such an asshole?' I asked, truly interested in his answer.

'It's in my nature,' he said and Luna laughed. Personally, I didn't see any humor in any of this.

'Maybe we should talk to that girl she was having lunch with,' I said. 'Maybe she said something incriminating to her.'

There was a loud sigh from the driver's position. '*You* need to give it a rest,' Champion said. 'One suspect at a time. Today's special is the vic's mom, OK?'

'OK, fine,' I said, gritting my teeth. 'She probably did it anyway.'

'Probably not,' Luna said.

'Then why are we doing this?' Champion asked, rather loudly.

Luna shrugged. 'What else do we have?'

Champion pointed behind him. 'Her kid,' he said.

I glared at his back, hoping his hair would spontaneously combust.

Graham kept his eyes on the mom, although trying to be coy about it. It didn't take long for her to find what she was looking for, and, as Champion had surmised, she put the thing she found in her right front coat pocket. Check, Graham thought to himself. Over and out.

'Let's go,' Adrianne Alexander said, moving to the door, Graham following. She opened the door with the obvious intent of peeking out to see if anyone was there but the door was pushed open by the detective, making Ms Alexander stumble backward.

'What's going on here?' Champion demanded, with Graham thinking *not Hollywood, but not bad.*

'Ah—' Graham stammered.

Ms Alexander righted herself, squaring her shoulders. 'I'm Bishop Alexander's mother and I have a right to my son's things,' she said.

'No, you don't,' Champion said. 'Not those things in a sealed room that could be considered evidence,' he continued, trying to ignore Graham's head repeatedly pointing in the direction of her right pocket. 'And you!' he said, turning on Graham in an attempt to get him to stop the head bobbing. 'What the hell do you think you're doing?'

'Ah, she asked—'

'Not another word!' Champion said. Then: 'Did either of you take anything out of here?'

'Of course not,' Ms Alexander said.

'Do you mind if I have a look?' he said, reaching for her left coat pocket, finding nothing then going for the right. He pulled out the photo he'd seen earlier in the lap drawer of the victim's desk. The picture of his parents in an embrace. 'What's this?'

'Nothing,' the woman said, her face turning pale as she spoke.

'Looks like something to me,' Champion said.

'Can I go now?' Graham asked.

'Shut up,' Champion said. 'Actually, yeah, you can go now. Straight to jail. Both of you! Come on!'

Luna showed up at that moment to help cuff the suspects, latching on to Graham to make sure the cuffs were loose on him.

'Don't you dare!' Adrianne Alexander said, pulling away from Champion. 'I want my attorney right this minute! You had no right to search my body—'

'I saw something incriminating sticking out of your pocket,' he said.

'That's bullshit, you son of a bitch!' she yelled as he got both her arms behind her and snapped on the cuffs.

'Yeah, that's what they call me,' he said, and, with Luna's help, walked his prisoners out of the room.

'I don't know who that is,' Lisa Garcia, the computer tech in the office said, 'but it's not her husband. According to what I could dig up on Adrianne Alexander, she's never been married. Alexander's her maiden name. And the vic's birth certificate says "father unknown."'

'She doesn't seem the type,' I said, although I'd been told talking was close to a criminal offense and I should keep my mouth shut.

Both Luna and Champion shot me a look, but Luna said, 'What type is that?'

'The type that would get knocked up and keep her baby. How old is she?' I asked Garcia.

'I'll ask the questions!' Champion said. Then sighed. 'How old is she?' he asked Garcia.

Lisa Garcia, attempting to hide a smile, said, 'Forty-nine.'

'OK,' I said. 'Say Bishop was the same age as Graham – twenty. Means she was twenty-eight or twenty-nine when she got knocked up. We know she's a high roller in the oil business, right?'

'There's only your son's word about that—' Champion started, but Garcia interrupted.

'No, she's right,' she said, looking at her computer screen. 'She's vice president of Legacy Oil Company, which is one of the big five. So, yeah, she's a high roller.'

'Education?' I asked.

She hit a few buttons, then said, 'Masters from the Wharton School of Economics.'

'So,' I concluded, 'she made a conscious decision to get pregnant.'

'What makes you say that?' Champion asked in an accusatory manner.

'A woman of her education, obvious ambition and sociopathic tendencies wouldn't keep an unwanted pregnancy. I think she was feeling the clock ticking – we felt it a lot earlier back in those days – and decided to get her a kid.' Turning to Garcia, I asked, 'She's the natural mother according to the birth certificate?'

She clicked back to another screen and said, 'That's what it says.'

'So she either duped some guy into getting her pregnant without knowing he was doing it or she went for artificial insemination,' I said.

'OK, but what does that have to do with anything?' Champion demanded.

'That picture. It's not daddy,' Luna said.

'Oh,' Champion said. Then he got up and headed for the interrogation rooms.

Luna allowed me to follow her into the observation room to watch Champion interrogate Adrianne Alexander. Well, she didn't so much allow me as didn't notice I was there until after the door was closed behind us. She just sighed and didn't say anything.

Champion held the picture up in front of Ms Alexander. 'Who's this?' he asked.

'None of your business,' she said. Then added: 'Where's my lawyer?'

'Have you called him?' Champion asked.

'Of course not! You haven't let me near a phone!'

'Then I guess he's not here yet,' Champion said.

Alexander jumped to her feet. 'Look, you pissant—'

'Sit down right now!' Champion said.

She stood there for thirty seconds or so then slowly sat back down. 'I'm not saying a word.'

'That's five,' he said.

'That's the last!'

'That's three.'

'What are you? Twelve?'

'Four. You're going back up.'

'Oh, for God's sake!' Alexander said, throwing her arms up in the air. 'What in God's name do you want?'

Champion pointed at the picture. 'Who's this?'

She folded her arms over her chest and looked over his head

at the mirror, about eye level with me. 'None of your business,' she said.

'Obviously it is,' Champion said. 'Why else would you rope the Pugh kid into sneaking you into your son's room when you knew it was off limits?'

'I had no idea it was off—'

'The seal on the door didn't give you a clue?'

'To me!' she finished. 'I'm his mother, for Christ's sake! I have a right to my son's things!'

'Actually, no, you don't. Not while they're in a sealed room and still considered possible evidence,' Champion reminded her.

She huffed. It wasn't a sigh. It was an actual huff. I've heard about them but never actually seen someone do it. It wasn't pretty.

'I want to call my attorney now!' she said.

'You're not under arrest, Ms Alexander. You're only being detained as a possible witness. As such, you don't have the privilege of a telephone call.'

'Are you out of your mind?' she yelled, jumping again to her feet.

'You're acting somewhat irrationally, Ms Alexander. We have an arrangement with Austin State Home to detain people who are acting irrationally. Would you like me to call them?'

She sank back down on her chair. 'Are you threatening to have me locked up in a mental institution? Are you really doing that?'

'Of course not!' Champion said. 'I'm just encouraging you not to act irrationally.'

'I'm going to have your badge!' she yelled. 'Do you have any idea who I am?'

'Yes, ma'am, you're the woman who broke into a sealed room and stole—'

'I'm senior vice president of Legacy Oil and as such I'm quite familiar with the governor *and* the attorney general! The attorney general and I play golf whenever he's in Houston! So if you don't want to end up out of a job and unemployable, I'd suggest you get me my goddam phone call *now*!'

'Actually, the attorney general is my brother-in-law,' Champion said, 'so that's not much of a threat. I know where his bodies are buried.' He grinned at her.

I turned to Luna. 'Really? His brother-in-law?'

Luna shook her head. 'Not that I've ever heard. It's OK to lie when interrogating a suspect and I'm pretty sure that's what Nate is doing.'

'I hate it when you call him by his first name,' I said – OK, peckishly.

'Shut up,' she said.

I turned my attention back to the interrogation room.

'One more time,' Champion said, poking his finger forcefully on the picture before him. 'Who is this?'

'I'm not telling you! Lock me up! Whatever!' Alexander said, arms across her chest, her eyes again looking anywhere but at Champion.

'OK, fine. If that's what you want.' He went to the door and opened it, calling to a uniformed officer, 'Hey, Minnie, I need you to take this lady down to lock-up. Material witness,' he said.

The officer named Minnie, a Hispanic woman in her thirties, came in and took Adrianne Alexander by the arm. Adrianne jerked her arm out of the woman's grasp, but when the younger woman brought out the cuffs, Alexander said, 'OK! All right! Jesus, you people!' and allowed herself to be led out of the interrogation room.

The door to the observation room opened and Champion walked in. Upon seeing me, he frowned deeply. 'Luna, I swear to God! What is this woman doing in here?'

Luna shrugged. 'She followed me,' she said.

'She's not a damn puppy!' Champion almost yelled.

'But I'm as cute as one,' I interjected. Nobody seemed to find it amusing.

I could see Champion physically trying to calm himself: deep breaths, rolling his shoulders, shaking out his arms. I have that effect on men. Finally, with a deep sigh, he turned to Luna and said, 'So, what did you think?'

'I think maybe we should have your gal Garcia run a facial recognition on the guy in the picture.'

'I'm not sure there's enough of his face to do that,' Champion said.

'We can ask,' Luna suggested.

'Yeah.' Champion sighed. 'Whatever.' He was not a happy man.

Graham and Miranda were coming out of their government class when they saw Gretchen Morley deep in conversation with another young woman. The same woman, Graham was pretty sure, Gretchen had been sitting with at Threadgills when he and his mother were having lunch. He leaned into Miranda. 'Who's that with Gretchen Morley?' he asked.

Miranda cut her eyes at him. 'Graham, honey, dearest, I have no idea what this Gretchen bitch looks like!'

He put his hands on her shoulders and turned her so she would be facing the two women, his back to them. 'See the short Asian woman with the glasses? The blonde she's talking to is Gretchen. Do you know the other one?'

'The Asian? Yeah, actually, to be specific she's Vietnamese. Tina Ng. She's a T.A. For Professor Winston.'

'She's too young to be a T.A. What is she, twelve?'

'Actually, she's like in her mid-twenties. She just looks young,' Miranda said.

'Can you tell what they're talking about?' he asked, whispering.

'No,' Miranda whispered back. 'I don't read lips.'

'So get closer,' Graham said. 'I'll step back inside the class-room so Gretchen won't see me. Act like you're reading an assignment or something.'

Miranda shook her head. 'Boy, you are just a load of laughs, aren't you, Pugh?'

'Please?'

She grinned. 'Nancy Drew at your service!' she said and headed down the hall, past the two women to the bulletin board only a foot or so away from them, and began to peruse the notices.

Graham snuck back into the classroom he'd just vacated. It was empty so he had no problem propping up a wall as he waited. In about five minutes he saw Gretchen Morley pass the classroom where he was hiding. A minute or two after that, Miranda was by his side.

'Well?' he asked.

She shook her head. 'Couldn't really understand what they were talking about but I took notes, hoping you'd know.'

'OK, let me see!'

She pulled her notepad away from him. 'It's in my shorthand. No way you can read it. Or anybody, for that matter.' She bent over it. 'Let me see, now, I think, no, maybe it says—'

'Anybody includes you?' Graham asked.

'Shush. OK. She – Ng – said, "Not tonight, it's too soon," then Gretchen said, "I can't keep it," then Ng said, "Just shut up and do what I tell you," then Gretchen started to cry—'

'Are you serious?'

'Yes, I am. Big old fat tears falling out of her eyes. In my world, we call that crying.'

'God, you're a smartass.'

She grinned. 'And you like that,' she said.

Graham grinned back. 'Actually, yeah, I kinda do.' Then he shook himself. 'OK, what happened after she started crying?'

'Ng said, "Try to control yourself, you blithering idiot."'

'Blithering idiot? Really? I've heard my grandpa use that term but no one younger than their mid-seventies!'

'I can't help you with that. That's what she said. I had to actually write down "blithering" because I couldn't come up with a shorthand way of writing it.'

'OK,' Graham said, 'so then what?'

'Ng goes, "If you can't handle this, Morley, I'll find someone who can!" Real mean, like.'

'What did Gretchen say?'

'She calmed down rather quickly, I thought, and said, "Of course I can handle it! You can count on me!" I thought she was going to burst into song for a moment there,' Miranda said.

'Song?' Graham asked.

Miranda rolled her eyes. 'You've never seen *Toy Story*? "You've Got A Friend In Me"?'

'Oh, right, whatever. And then?' Graham asked.

Miranda shrugged. 'She left – Gretchen did.'

'I saw her go by the door,' Graham said.

'Yeah, well she came this way and Ng went the other way. And that was that.'

Graham put his arm around Miranda and kissed her solidly on the lips. 'Good job, Nancy,' he said.

'We're really not going to play fantasy sex games, are we? Me Nancy, you Ned?'

'Who's Ned?'

Miranda sighed. 'Nancy Drew's boyfriend, dumbass!'

'How would I know?' he answered, wounded. 'Nancy Drew's a girl's book. I don't read girl's books.'

Miranda shook her head as they left the classroom. 'I'm going to have a talk with your mother,' she said.

'Oh, yeah, we need to tell her and Luna what you overheard,' Graham said.

'That too. But my main concern is your lack of feminist upbringing! Your mother has something to answer for!'

'Oh, don't!' Graham said, almost begging. 'Anything but that! Please!'

Miranda laughed and took his hand. Graham wasn't sure what that meant.

ELEVEN

L isa Garcia found Champion and his two female companions in his cubicle. 'Didn't have to do too much to find out who this guy is,' she said, throwing down a poster. It was obviously the guy in the picture with Adrianne Alexander, being overly intimate. The poster she threw down contained another picture of the guy, with another woman and three kids. All holding up two fingers in a 'V' for victory sign. And under the picture was the legend 'Vote for Al! Next US Senator from the State of Texas!'

'Shit,' Champion said. 'It *is* Al Nelsley! Damn!'

'He's that Republican asshole running for senate!' the Pugh woman said.

'She's a left-wing pinko liberal,' Luna informed Champion with a grin.

'Shit, that's all I need,' Champion said under his breath.

'So, with his white-bread wife and his three blonde offspring right there, why is he canoodling with Bishop's – excuse the expression – mother?' Pugh asked.

'Because he's an asshole politician and they all screw around?' Luna suggested.

Pugh shrugged. 'You have a point. But I thought Republicans were the ones who couldn't keep their hands out of your pockets. Democrats are traditionally the ones that can't keep their hands out of their own pants.'

'I haven't voted in twenty years,' Champion said, 'so this discussion is boring me. They're all assholes. Let's move on.'

Both Luna and Pugh stared at him, speechless. Finally, Luna said, 'Twenty years?'

He shrugged. 'Maybe longer.' He looked up at Pugh and grinned. 'When Reagan couldn't run anymore, I quit voting.'

'Oh my God!' Pugh said and shuddered.

'Right,' Luna said. 'OK. Let's move on. So why would Bishop

have a picture of his mother and the senator-wannabe canoodling, as Pugh put it?'

'Blackmail,' Pugh said, and both Champion and Luna looked
at her with raised eyebrows. 'Seriously. From what Graham
has told us,' she said, indicating Luna, 'Bishop was always
calling her for money, even though she sent him nearly a
thousand a month. So, say, during winter break, he finds this
picture, knows who Nelsley is and decides that's a good way
of getting more cash.'

Luna was nodding but Champion wasn't about to give the
mom that kind of satisfaction. 'So you think she killed the
kid for that picture? Why didn't she just take it when she was
in there stabbing her son? Which, in truth, I just don't believe.'

Pugh sank back in the chair. 'Me neither, to be truthful. But
maybe that's just because I'm a mom and can't fathom such
things.' She brightened. 'But it happens!' she added.

'I'm not buying it,' Luna said. 'I think when she found out
her son was dead, she was worried that someone would find
the picture. That's why she had Graham break in.'

Pugh's shoulders began to sag. 'Maybe,' she said grudgingly.

'Which brings us back to your kid,' Champion said.

I don't like to use that nasty four-letter word 'hate,' but at that
moment I hated Nate Champion with every fiber of my being.
He was seriously going after my kid – again! No one would
believe the truth, that: 1. Graham didn't have a *real* reason
for killing Bishop, and 2. Graham didn't have it in him to do
such a thing. Neither was something Champion was going to
buy. Unfortunately, my son had: a motive, such as it was;
means – the cafeteria was full of knives; and the opportunity
– he was in the room when Bishop was murdered. I was getting
seriously scared.

I'd been riding the coattails of both Champion and Luna
this entire time, I thought. It was time I went out on my own,
since I was the only one who believed Graham was truly
innocent.

I stood up from the rolling chair I'd been allocated and said,
'Look, y'all, I have a splitting headache. I think I'll head back
to the hotel. It's Advil time.'

Luna stood, too. 'I'll drive you back.'

'No, no,' I said, pushing her lightly back in her seat. 'You stay and try to figure this crap out. I'll grab a cab.'

'You sure?' Luna said.

'Leave the woman alone, Elena,' Champion said.

I still hated him but for once he was – unknowingly – on my side. I waved and headed out of the office. Once on the street, I used my cell phone to call Graham.

'Where are you?' I asked when he answered.

'Ah, around,' he said.

'I need you to pick me up,' I said.

'I'm kinda busy, Mom.'

'Doing what?'

'Don't listen to him, Mrs Pugh!' came a female voice, obviously in Graham's car.

'Is that Miranda?' I asked.

'Maybe,' he said.

'We're coming to get you!' the female voice said.

'Well, Miranda's certainly more polite than you! Which isn't saying much. I'm at the police station. On the sidewalk. Make it snappy,' I said and hung up.

'I'm glad she left,' Champion said to Luna.

'Don't be,' Luna said.

'Why?'

'Because she's up to something. I know that woman like the back of my hand. She doesn't do cabs and she doesn't turn down a ride. So she's up to something. And that's never a good sign.'

Champion stared at Luna for a moment, then said, 'Should we go get her?' It was obvious that this wasn't his favorite plan.

Luna shrugged. 'Too late now, probably. She's wiley. Like a coyote.'

'Funny.'

Luna noticed he wasn't laughing, or even smiling for that matter.

'So what do we do now?' she asked him.

'Arrest the Pugh kid,' Champion answered.

'No.'

Champion sighed. 'Look, I've got motive and opportunity. As far as means, that's not a problem. The kid's good for this, Elena.'

'So's Gretchen Morley. And Lexie Thurgood. And Bobby Dunston! Not to mention Gaylord Fuchs! I mean, the list of possibles is as long as your arm, for crying out loud!'

'Yeah, but we have no proof that any of those people were there in the room when the kid was murdered. Pugh was!'

'And he was unconscious! Which we would know if you'd done your due diligence and taken his blood the next morning!'

'Hey, he was a smoking gun! There was no call to test his blood—'

'Bullshit!'

They both stopped talking and just looked at each for a long moment. Finally, Champion said, 'I guess we'll just have to agree to disagree.'

Luna shook her head. 'You're railroading this kid, Nate, and I won't stand for it. I'll do what I have to do to prove you wrong.' She stood up to leave.

Champion stood to face her. 'Don't get in my way, Elena. This isn't your jurisdiction. I've let you tag along out of respect for you as a colleague, but I won't stand for your interference.'

'Nice seeing you, Nate. Have a nice life,' Luna said and headed out of the squad room.

Graham picked me up on the sidewalk outside the police station. Miranda, who was in the front passenger seat, crawled into the back, letting me ride shotgun. I climbed in and turned to Miranda.

'How's he doing?' I asked, pointing my head at my son, who was scowling behind the wheel.

'Other than terrified of the two of us getting together? Pretty much OK,' she said.

I looked at Graham. I think I liked this girl. But I'd liked all the girls my son had become involved with, which said something about Graham's good taste. How long would this one hang around? Once Graham got arrested for killing his roommate. Once he went on trial. Once he ended up in prison.

I turned around and stared out the front window.

'Mom?' he said.

'Um,' I said.

'What's up?'

'They don't like Bishop's mother for the kill,' I said.

'I'm still their best fit,' he said. It wasn't a question so I didn't answer it.

'That's bullshit!' Miranda said from the back seat. 'Excuse my language, Mrs Pugh.'

'Where do you think I learned to cuss like a sailor?' Graham said.

'From your father,' I threw in, then turned to Miranda. 'Call me E.J.,' I said. 'This is getting too dicey for formalities.'

'Yeah, I guess so,' she said, her voice dejected. 'But you know he didn't do it?' she asked.

'Of course I know that!' I said, my voice rising. Who the hell did she think I was, anyway? Jeez.

'Ah, I'm sorry,' she said. 'This is just weird.'

'Look,' Graham said, his eyes squarely on the road, 'Miranda, I'm taking you back to your dorm. You don't need to be involved in this—'

'Try it and see how far you get!' she said. 'I'm in this for the long haul. If necessary, I'll learn to bake so I can put a file in a cake to take to you in prison!'

Graham and 1 looked at each other and began to laugh. I think we were both on the verge of hysterics, but I was able to stop myself before the tears began.

Champion was pissed. How dare Luna talk to him like that? This was his case and he could arrest whomever he wanted to arrest! She needed to get her ass back to Hicksville, USA, where she came from and leave him alone. But, deep down, he wondered about a couple of things: like why there was no blood on the kid the next morning, on or around him. And why in the hell didn't he, Champion, test the kid's blood? Yeah, it wasn't exactly protocol but it wasn't unheard of either. The kid could have been on drugs – like PCP. That shit has caused more than one college student to go berserk.

And did he believe what the Morley girl had said about the

kid sitting up in the middle of the night and staring at the vic? She could be lying about that for reasons of her own. Or the vic could have lied to her – for reasons of his own. But why? OK, he thought. The vic might have been trying to impress Morley in some weird way. *Hey, look at me! I'm so cool my roommate wants to kill me.* Or, more likely – maybe – Morley wanted to take any heat off her and put it on the Pugh kid. He was pretty sure she lied about keying the vic's car and the Ex-Lax brownies. But would she need more revenge than that for the end of a three-week affair? Who knew, he thought. Women were weird. You never knew what was going to set one off. He had first-hand knowledge of that: hence, the divorce.

She said he forgot their anniversary three years in a row; *she* said he left his underwear everywhere but the hamper; *she* said he wasn't romantic. *Romantic*, for God's sake! After twenty-eight years of marriage, what was there to be romantic about? Were those actual reasons to file for divorce? He didn't think so. He wondered how long this new guy was going to be *romantic*. Give him a month and that would be that. Guys only got romantic to get in a woman's drawers, Champion figured, and once they got in, what was the point? It was like dancing. You danced with a woman so you could hold her body close, maybe put your hand on her ass. Once you got her into bed, what would be the reason to go dancing? But they *always* wanted to go dancing!

Enough, he told himself. The case. The goddamn case. Put your mind on that. Shit, just go get that Pugh kid and lock him up. He got up from his desk and headed to his car.

'So we need to work this thing on our own,' I told Graham. And Miranda, I guess. I mean, she was there.

'I like that Morley bitch,' Miranda said. 'Graham, did you tell your mom what I overheard?'

'No—' he started, but I interrupted.

'What? Now!'

And so they told me about seeing her with the same young Asian woman Graham and I had seen her with at Threadgills. And the conversation.

'That doesn't sound good,' I said. 'As in they were up to something, which is good. But that something was probably no good—'

'Right,' Graham said. 'We got it. It's good and not good.'

'Graham! Don't talk to your mother like that!'

OK, I wasn't thrilled about this girl – excuse me, woman – defending me from my son. I've had plenty of practice doing that myself. Ignoring her, I said, 'No, it's not good. But what is it?'

'Morley has something she doesn't want to keep,' Miranda said. 'But that Ng woman wants her to keep it and sort of threatened her. Then Morley backed down.'

'So what is it Ng wanted Morley to keep?' Graham asked.

Miranda shrugged, but only I could see her. I said, 'I'd like to find that out. Let's go see little Miss Gretchen.'

'Without Luna?' my son asked.

'Definitely without Luna,' I said.

We caught Gretchen Morley coming out of her sorority house, a book satchel over her shoulder. Seeing us, she veered away, heading in the opposite direction. We hurried to catch up and she moved faster. We moved faster. She began to run. That's when I decided I really did like Miranda Wisher. She took off like a Dallas Cowboy and tackled Morley, book bag and all.

Graham and I rushed up to the two prone young women. 'What the hell?' Gretchen yelled, trying to untangle herself from Miranda's arms and legs. 'Who are you? And what the hell are you doing?'

Graham extended an arm to Morley and pulled her up. I helped Miranda up, who was grinning from ear to ear. I couldn't help but grin back.

Morley shook off Graham's hand and bent down to grab her satchel, hugging it close to her body. I had the somewhat insane idea that whatever Gretchen Morley had been told by the Ng woman to keep was in that satchel. I turned and whispered to Miranda, 'It's in the satchel.'

Miranda grabbed at it while Gretchen tugged back. I was afraid a full-scale tug of war would garner more attention than we needed, so I grabbed the satchel, too, and between us

Miranda and I were able to retrieve it from Morley.

'Give that back! Who the fuck do you think you people are?' Morley screamed.

'We need to see what's in the bag,' I said.

'You need a warrant to do that!' she screeched.

'No, we're not police,' I said.

'Then you're thieves and I'm calling the police!'

'You want them to see what's in the satchel?' I asked.

'Mom—' Graham started.

I ignored him. 'Shall we have a look?' I said, going for the bag's zipper.

'Pugh, you really shouldn't do that,' came a voice I recognized but really didn't want to hear.

My shoulders slumped and I turned around to find Luna standing there. 'Look,' I said, 'she's hiding something and I want to know what it is!'

'Maybe it's that Advil you were so anxious to take?' she said.

I started unzipping the bag. Luna put her hand over mine. 'Anything you find in there will not be admissible in a court of law, Pugh. You know that.'

'Oh, for God's sake!' Gretchen Morley said. She grabbed the bag out of my hands and unzipped it, spilling the contents on the sidewalk in front of her dorm. 'There! Happy?'

I squatted down to look. Books. A laptop computer. A hair fixer. And a protein bar. That was it.

'Let's go, Pugh.'

'Yeah, why don't you all go?' Gretchen Morley said. 'Straight to hell!' With that she picked up her belongings and scooped them into the satchel. But not before I saw the zippered compartment on the inside of the bag – the compartment that she hadn't opened.

'So what's got the bug up your butt about Morley again?' Luna asked.

We told her – Graham and I – about seeing her and Ng together at Threadgills, and Miranda about the conversation she heard between Morley and Ng in the hall of the chemistry building.

'Ng?' Luna asked, a frown on her face. 'Tina Ng?'

'Yes!' Miranda said.

'A teaching assistant, right?' Luna asked.

'Yes! Miranda said, almost jumping up and down.

I looked at Luna. 'What do you know about her?' I asked.

'Champion interviewed her—' Luna started but Miranda interrupted.

'I told you there was something going on there!'

'About what?' I asked Luna, ignoring Miranda, who, let's face it, was fairly hard to ignore. But I tried.

'She was the T.A. for the class that Lexie Thurgood said the girl who told her about Bobby Dunston's parents was in.'

'What's that got to do with anything?' Graham asked.

We all shrugged. 'Damned if I know,' Luna said. 'But it's a string. Now we've just got to pull it.'

The Pugh kid wasn't at the motel. Neither was his mom or Luna. Champion sat in his unmarked and waited, thinking. What did he actually have on the kid? How easily could that lawyer, Stuart Freeman, get him out of jail? Pretty damn quick was the answer to that. Did he shoot his wad now or wait for more confirmation? Surely it was coming. The kid did it, he knew that. Probably. More than likely. Maybe.

In frustration, Champion hit the steering wheel with the palm of his hand – hard. It accomplished two things: he hurt his hand and the horn of the five-year-old unmarked began to beep and wouldn't stop. Cursing, Champion got out of the car and opened the hood, taking note that the motel manager and several guests were outside now and staring at him, with some idiot shouting, 'Turn it off!' at the top of his lungs. In a perfect world, Champion thought, he could throw the guy's ass in jail for that.

He started pulling wires until the horn stopped, but then, once in the car, he couldn't get it to start. He knew nothing about cars except how to put gas in them. And he'd been pissed when full-service stations had mostly shut down and he'd had to learn how to pump it himself. His wife – ex-wife, he reminded himself – could change her own oil. And often, jokingly – he was told repeatedly – called him a sissy. He kind of wished she was around now so she could do something about it. Instead, he used his cell phone and called for service from the police garage. He knew he was going to get harassed for it but at this point he didn't care. He just wanted to arrest somebody. Anybody would do.

TWELVE

I missed my overlarge tub in my renovated bathroom back home. But the one in the motel room worked in a pinch. I'm a water baby; I think best while in water. So I lay there in the small motel bathtub, turning the hot water on occasionally to keep things all toasty, and thought about my life in its current state. My husband and three of my children were away from me, doing God only knows what, while I was stuck in a motel room with a cranky cop and my son was next door doing God only knows what with his new girlfriend. And all of this was just a waiting game. Waiting for Champion to either arrest my son or find the real killer. Somehow I didn't think he was even looking for the real killer.

My life had taken a drastic turn many years ago when my daughter Bess's birth family was murdered. They were our best friends, our two families entwined in so many ways that, with their passing, it seemed our whole world had collapsed. But Willis and I had persevered, gotten Bess and the rest of our family through it and had helped find out who had killed our friends. That was also when I met Elena Luna, who now lived in the house where Bess's birth family had lived. But their murders, and my involvement in the resolution of that, had started a trend in my life. A trend in finding dead bodies, or somehow getting involved in murder. But this was the first time since then it had truly hit home. The first time I was so scared I could hardly think straight.

And maybe that was the problem. I hadn't been thinking straight. There had to be a reason why Bishop Alexander was killed and my son roofied. No one would go to that much trouble and be that premeditated just because someone pissed them off. There was more to it. I knew there were two basic reasons for murder: love or money. As far as I could tell, the only person who could be considered to have *loved* (and I use that term loosely) Bishop was his ex-girlfriend, Gretchen

Morley. And with her 'love' probably meant what the man in question could do for her. Money, connections, power of some sort. Well, Bishop had a couple of those things – money and connections – but they were second hand, through his mother. Morley would have to wait a while to get her hands on any of that. And for all I knew, Morley herself came from a rich family and didn't need those things. She *was* pissed enough to key his car and send him those Ex-Lax brownies, but I didn't feel the passion coming from her. There would have to be passion to kill someone over love.

And the love angle could also be considered as a motive for the student adviser, Gaylord Fuchs. Bishop had acted horribly toward Fuchs' wife, so horribly that Fuchs had taken a swing at him. It hadn't worked, mainly because of Fuchs' size. Would those two humiliations have been enough for Fuchs to plan such a brutal revenge? Wouldn't Graham have noticed a little person in the cafeteria? Probably not. I had to admit my son was pretty oblivious most of the time.

And we hadn't even started on Bobby Dunston's parents. Had Champion interviewed them? I was pretty sure Luna hadn't or she would have said something. Did we go talk with them? Where were they? I wondered. Where did Bobby come from?

The only person left was Lexie Thurgood and Luna had mostly written her off. She was definitely a long shot.

As the water began to get cold – so cold another shot of the hot water wouldn't help much – I decided to get out of the tub. I was getting a prune look anyway. I took one of the motel's skimpy towels and dried off as best I could, then tucked myself into my thick terrycloth robe I'd brought with me and went back into the main room. Luna started talking before I was totally in the room.

'So instead of going after Morley again,' Luna suggested, 'why don't I go visit Tina Ng?'

'"I"? As in singular? As in you go and I sit here in the motel and twiddle my thumbs?' I said. 'No. *Nada. Nien.* Been there, done that. I'm going with you!'

'And so are we!' said Miranda Wisher from the doorway. I hadn't heard her and Graham enter my room.

'Absolutely not!' Luna said. She sighed. 'I'll take E.J. but the two of you are to stay here, do you understand?'

'How about we follow in my car?' Graham suggested. 'And just wait for you outside?'

'Why? We'll come back here and tell you what happened!' Luna said.

'Yeah, maybe you will,' Miranda said, 'and maybe you won't.'

'You don't trust me?' Luna said.

The 'no' was unanimous from all three of us standing there.

Luna looked indignant. 'Maybe I should just go home – back to Black Cat Ridge. I came here to help you, Pugh, but if you don't need it—'

'Don't get your knickers in a knot, Luna,' I said. 'I need your help. *We* need your help. But we have to be sure you're on Graham's side and you're not going to go running off to Champion about everything we do!'

'I haven't—' she started, then stopped. 'OK, I won't. Nate and I aren't exactly on speaking terms right now anyway.'

I tilted my head in a question. 'Why not?'

She shrugged. 'I sorta suggested he was an idiot because of the way he's been handling this whole thing. He seemed to take exception to that.'

I wanted to hug her. But Luna and I – we don't hug. Instead, I held up my hand. She just looked at it. 'High five?' I said. She ignored me. I stood there for what seemed an eternity before Miranda ran up and hit my palm with hers. Somehow, it just wasn't the same thing.

'Where does Ng live?' Luna asked.

'Graham, where's your laptop?' Miranda asked.

'In my room.'

Miranda grabbed my son's arm and headed for the door. 'We'll find out!' she said over her shoulder.

Once in Luna's car, I brought up what I'd been thinking about in the tub. 'We haven't talked to Bobby Dunston's parents.'

'True,' she said.

'Don't you think we should?'

She shrugged. 'Do you really think they're viable?'

'I don't know!' I said, more heatedly than I'd intended.

'Don't yell at me, Pugh!' Luna shot back.

'I'm not yelling at you!' I yelled at her.

'Yes, you are!' she yelled back.

'I'm yelling at the situation! Not you!' I yelled.

'Well, whatever you're yelling at, stop it!' she yelled.

'OK!' I yelled.

We were quiet for a moment, although the small motel room seemed to vibrate from the strength of our voices.

'They're people we haven't talked to yet,' I said in a reasonable voice.

'You're right. We haven't talked to them,' she said.

'Has Champion?' I asked.

She shrugged. 'I don't know. I doubt at this point that he'd tell me.'

'Do we know where they live? Where Bobby's from?'

'I don't. Do you?'

'No, of course not!' There I went, almost yelling again. I took a deep breath and said quietly, 'But Miranda seems to do well on the computer. Why don't we ask her to look up his home address?'

She nodded. 'Doable. But first, let's check out this Ng chick.'

I sighed. One problem at a time, I told myself. One witness at a time.

Champion had no idea where to go next to find the kid, short of putting out an APB on him, and he didn't have enough to do that. Hell, he really didn't have enough to do much of anything. His case was weaker than a wet Kleenex. He decided to go back to the shop and review the whole thing. There had to be something he was missing. A smoking gun – or in this case knife – that would put the Pugh kid away for good.

Tina Ng was home when we got there. It was the bottom floor of a fourplex close to campus and appeared to be a one-bedroom, although Ng didn't bother to give us a tour. Peeking in, I could see the place was furnished in IKEA – everything in it I'd seen in an IKEA catalog, from the furniture to knick-knacks to the dishes draining in the IKEA wooden dish drainer.

Luna and I had left Graham and Miranda at the bagel shop on the drag, just a few blocks from Ng's apartment. The plan was to regroup there after we'd interviewed the T.A. To say she wasn't pleased to see us would be inappropriate. She was totally non-committal, as in she said nothing after Luna introduced herself and showed her credentials. Ng just stood there looking at us. Her eyes gave away nothing. No fear, no anger, no humor – not much of anything.

'May we come in?' Luna finally asked.

'Why?' Ng said.

'We need to talk, unless you want to answer questions here in the hall,' Luna said.

Ng shrugged but still said nothing. She just turned, leaving the door open – her way, I suppose, of inviting us in. She sat down on an IKEA chair while Luna and I chose the IKEA sofa. Little choice really, since those two things – the chair and the sofa – were the only places to sit in the room.

And again, our hostess said not a word. Luna broke the silence. 'I need to speak to you about Gretchen Morley.'

No answer.

'Do you know Gretchen Morley?' Luna asked.

'Yes.'

'How long have you known her?'

Ng shrugged. Luna decided to play the silent game herself. Finally Ng said, 'Since her freshman year. Maybe two years.'

'How did you come to know her?'

'She was in the economics class I teach.'

'Is she still in one of your classes?' Luna asked.

'No.'

'But you still see her?'

'Yes.'

'Are you friends?'

There was another silence, then Ng said, 'Yes,' but it was tentative – the first time I thought she'd actually lied.

'So what is she holding for you?' Luna said.

I stared hard at Ng, waiting for some giveaway. Eyes shifting, posture tightening. Anything. But I got nothing. Ng just sat there, not answering.

'Ms Ng?' Luna said. 'Could you answer my question?'

'No.'

'Why not?'

'I don't know what you mean, so therefore I see no reason to answer,' Ng said.

'OK, then let me explain. You were overheard this morning during a conversation with Gretchen Morley, in which she reportedly stated that she didn't want to keep something and you reportedly told her she had to. I just want to know what that something is.'

'No.'

'Pardon?'

'Someone lied. I said nothing like that to Gretchen Morley.'

'Really?'

No answer.

'Ms Ng, you're not being very cooperative.'

Ng stood up and walked to the bar that separated the kitchen from the living room of her apartment. She went to a very nice IKEA bowl I'd thought about buying for Graham for his dorm room and brought out a card. Coming back into the living room, she handed the card to Luna.

'Talk to her,' she said.

Luna looked at the card. 'Is this your attorney?'

'Yes.' Ng turned, walked to the door and opened it. She didn't say anything. She didn't have to. We got up and left.

Champion was headed to McMillan Hall, thinking maybe the Pugh kid decided to go back to the scene of the crime. Hey, he reminded himself, it's happened! He was driving down Guadalupe Street, better known in that section in front of campus as the drag, when he was stopped at a red light. Sitting there, he happened to glance in the window of the bagel shop across from the entrance to the university. He almost spit out his nicotine gum when he saw Luna, the mom, the kid and some other chick sitting there big as life. He looked around for a parking space but, of course, there weren't any.

'So you think she's lying?' Graham reiterated.

'Yep,' I said.

'Probably,' Luna said. 'Her demeanor changed when I asked

her if she and Morley were friends. And then she basically clammed up when asked about what Morley was keeping for her.'

'Of course, clamming up seems to be her *modus operandi*,' I said.

Luna nodded. 'I'd say she's the strong, silent type for sure.'

'But she's so little!' Miranda said.

Luna cut her eyes at the girl. 'I meant that figuratively.'

'Oh,' Miranda said, and I saw Graham touch her hand. I could only hope this one lasted for more than a few months. I had to wonder about the reasons my son seemed to flit about between women. Was I giving him way too much credit in thinking he'd broken up with Alicia to save her pain? Probably, I thought, and then felt guilty. Worry about one thing at a time, I told myself.

'What about Bobby Dunston's parents?' I asked Luna.

She sighed and my dander got up again, then I worried I'd start yelling in the bagel shop. Not good for my son's reputation, I told myself. If it didn't get totally ruined by, you know, being accused of murder and all.

'*What* about Bobby's parents?' Graham asked.

Calming myself, with great effort, I said, 'We haven't interviewed them yet. It may be a long shot but I think we should do it. Do you know where Bobby's from?'

'Ah, San Antonio, I think,' Graham said.

'Where's your laptop?' Miranda asked.

Sighing, Graham held out his keys. 'In the car,' he said and rolled his eyes.

'He's a caution, as my grandma used to say,' Miranda said, grinned at me and headed out the door.

'Where are you parked?' I asked Graham.

'Hell and gone,' he said.

The door to the bagel shop opened and we were blessed with the presence of Detective Champion. Yes, I'm using sarcasm.

'Well, hello!' he said upon seeing us, like it was a great big accident that he happened to walk into the same establishment where we were sitting – right in front of the big plate-glass window.

'Nate,' Luna said, nodding her head at him.

'Mind if I join you?' he asked, grabbing a chair from the next table.

'Yes!' Graham and I said, almost in unison.

Luna gave us all a look and said, 'Of course not. Please do.'

He pulled the chair up and sat down, resting his elbows on the table. 'So, what have you guys been up to?' he asked, with what passed – for him – as a pleasant expression on his face.

We were all as silent as Tina Ng.

'Did you want to get something to eat or drink?' Luna asked, pointing at the walk-up counter just as Miranda walked in carrying Graham's laptop and his keys.

She walked up to the table, handed Graham his things and stared daggers at Champion.

'Yeah,' he said then pointed at Miranda. 'Honey, you wanna go get me a cup of coffee? Black.'

'Get it yourself!' she said.

Luna looked at her and nodded her head toward the counter. Miranda sighed and headed that direction.

'Why are you here, Nate?' Luna asked once Miranda was out of earshot.

'To be truthful, I saw all y'all sitting here like a happy little family and I thought I'd just join in the fun.'

'Yeah, I'm buying that,' Luna said.

'Actually,' Champion said, turning to look directly at my son, 'I've been looking for y'all. Well, maybe not y'all, but him.'

'Leave him alone—' I started but Luna interrupted.

'If you're ready to charge Graham, please let us know so we can contact his attorney to meet us at the station. And of course, Mrs Pugh will have to release some funds for his bail—'

'If I were to charge him, it would be a capital offense. No bail on a capital offense.'

'I think Stuart Freeman could make a case for it,' Luna suggested.

Everyone was being so damn civil I was about to scream. Then Miranda came back with a cardboard cup of coffee – sans lid – and plopped it down hard in front of Champion. The hot liquid shot out and onto one of his hands. He yelped and grabbed the hand, and I had to press my own hand over my mouth to keep from laughing out loud. Miranda sat down next to me and we managed a hidden low five.

'You did that on purpose!' Champion spat at Miranda.

She did the big doe-eye routine and said, 'I'm so sorry! It was truly an accident.'

'Like hell!' he said but mostly under his breath. I don't think he intended to press the issue.

He stood up from the table, knocking his chair backwards. 'Look, I'm not charging him now but I want to know where he is at all times, you got that, Luna? No running around interviewing witnesses or going into his off-limits dorm room—'

'You were the one who sent me in there!' Graham said.

'Well, just don't do it again.'

'Is the city going to reimburse me for an outlay on new clothes?' I asked sweetly. 'He's been in the same ones since Monday and he's beginning to stink.'

'Mom!'

Champion looked from me to Graham to Luna and back to me. Then he sighed. 'Come on. Just you two. I'll let you into the room but just know I'm going to search everything you take out of there! Do you understand that?'

'Pretty much,' Graham said, trying hard to suppress a smile. He didn't succeed.

Champion had a good arrest and conviction record, maybe the best in the department. So he wasn't happy with what was going on with the Bishop Alexander case. The guy was such an asshole, Champion thought, that there were probably a long line of good suspects; he just didn't know all of them. The ones he had – the mother, the best buddy, the ex-girlfriend, the student adviser and the roommate – especially the room-mate – weren't that great. He was really running out of steam on the Pugh kid. He was almost certain now that he didn't do it. He was also almost certain that he really should have tested the kid's blood the morning they found the body. Yeah, it was convenient that he came up with all the symptoms of being roofied *after* Luna brought it up. But, then, that could be legit.

What kid his age pays that much attention to how he's feeling? You're tired, you sleep. You're hungry, you eat. You're horny, well, you do something about that, too, one way or another. But taking the time to figure out that you're sleepier than you would usually be, and groggier in the morning than you usually are, isn't something you think about when you're in college. Most kids would just think *what did I do last night?* and blame it on any substance he might have imbibed, be it liquid or of a more pharmaceutical nature. So, yeah. Here he was, Detective Superman, clearing his most promising witness. And taking him to the scene of the crime, for crying out loud.

Champion sighed as he opened the door to McMillan Hall for the kid and his mother. He sighed when he hit the button on the elevator for the fourth floor. He sighed when he used his pocket knife to cut the seal on the kid's dorm room door. And he sighed when he opened said door.

'I'm sorry this is so painful for you,' the kid's mother said, although he thought it was said with just a touch of sarcasm.

'You don't know the half of it,' Champion replied.

He stood against the door while mother and son went about packing up. And all he could do was watch.

'Don't worry about the stuff in the bathroom,' I said to Graham. 'We've already replaced most of that.'

'Ah, yeah, well, not everything,' my son said, blushed and moved into the bathroom, shutting the door behind him, which aroused the good detective's suspicions. I kind of giggled, thinking about Champion pushing the door open only to find Graham pocketing a wad of condoms. But the door to the bathroom opened before Champion could do anything and he settled back against the dorm room door, his steely eye watching Graham's every move. I wanted to say, 'Give it up, already!' but thought I'd let him keep his pride, such as it was.

We grabbed some sweatshirts, T-shirts, blue jeans, underwear and his heavy coat. He got his book bag and threw in some spiral notebooks and pens (not that he ever used them that I'd seen – he was of the age of 'if it doesn't go on the laptop it doesn't go.'). He then grabbed the pictures off his bureau of his sisters and his BFFs from high school, but Champion, ever the optimist, couldn't let that go.

'Just a minute,' he said, took the picture of Graham and his sisters and, taking the back off, examined it, put it back together, took the picture of Graham and his buds and did the same thing. There was no smoking gun hidden inside the picture frames. I could tell he was disappointed.

'Shall we go?' I asked the detective, using my smarmiest smile.

He opened the dorm room door and waved us through, sighing all the way back to the sidewalk.

'So we go to San Antonio,' I said to the room in general. Luna and I were sitting on my bed, Graham and Miranda on Luna's.

'I think you're being slightly ridiculous,' Luna said. 'That's a long way to go for a really iffy supposition. The chances the Dunstons had anything to do with this are slim to none.'

'I'm betting more on slim than none,' I said.

'And besides,' Miranda said, 'San Antonio's like an hour away. Maybe less. Google shows their address to be on the north side of town. Easy peasy.'

'We don't have time—'

'What else are we going to do?' I demanded. 'Sit here with our thumbs up our butts until Champion decides to arrest Graham? At least if we drive to San Antonio, even if the Dunstons are totally innocent, we'll get Graham out of harm's way.'

'The last thing Champion said was to let him know where Graham was at all times!' Luna said.

'Yeah, well, is he the boss of you?' I said, twisting a well-used phrase all my children had used more times than I care to remember.

'Pugh—'

'Luna.'

'God, Pugh,' she said, shaking her head.

'You got a better idea?' I asked.

She thought for a moment, took a deep breath and said, 'No.' Then she stood up and headed for the door. 'We'll take my car. And if anybody says anything – I mean *anything!* – to Champion about this, I'll have you for breakfast. With a side of toast!'

Graham had no idea why they were going to San Antonio. He figured Bobby's folks to be more than a long shot but he was happy to go. Being out of Champion's jurisdiction felt safer, somehow. Miranda had been right – it took less than an hour to get to the Dunstons' home. It was a nice Tara-looking thing, to Graham's eyes, with columns in the front, painted white with black shutters, and a lawn his dad would have killed for. St Augustine at least four inches thick, the sidewalk edging sharp as a well-creased pant leg. Having been the main lawn man at his home since the age of thirteen, Graham had an eye for a good lawn. Everything was brown, of course, due to winter and all, but the hedges were neatly squared while smaller ones were perfect little balls. He took out his phone and snapped some close-up shots. His dad would appreciate that. All three women turned and looked at him like he was crazy. He coughed slightly and put the phone back in the hip pocket of his clean jeans.

Luna rang the bell, and they could all hear the chimes inside playing a tune. He wasn't sure what it was but it sounded nice, he thought. The door was opened after a minute by a very large woman in a muumuu.

'Yes?' she said, staring at them with a furrowed brow.

Luna showed her badge. 'Mrs Dunston?'

'Yes? What is it?'

'I'm a consultant with the Austin police depart—'

The woman grabbed her heart and fell against the doorjamb. 'Oh my God! Robert! My baby! He's dead, isn't he?'

Luna grabbed the woman to keep her from falling. 'No, ma'am! I'm so sorry. No, your son is fine. It's about his friend, Bishop Alexander.'

The woman straightened and the furrowed brow deepened into a frown. 'That you-know-what!' she said through gritted teeth. 'Has he hurt my boy? I'm going to kill—'

'Ma'am, may we come in?' Luna said, rubbing her arms through her coat. 'It's chilly out here.'

'I'm sorry,' she said, although Graham thought she'd didn't look sorry. 'Yes, of course you may. But only if you're here to tell me that you-know-what has been thrown out of school!' she said, turning and walking into the room. 'I told Robert that boy was trouble with a capital T, but would he listen?' she said as they followed her past a fancy living room into a crowded family room. To Graham's eye, there was way too much furniture, and the fire in the fireplace, along with the central heating, made him want to strip off most of his clothes. 'Do y'all want something to drink? The coffee pot is mostly full.'

'Water,' Graham choked. 'Please.'

Mrs Dunston pointed to the kitchen just beyond the family room. 'There's bottled water in the fridge. Help yourself,' she said, lowering herself onto a dark red sofa, half of which was covered with a brown throw sprouting more dog hair than one would think possible. Unless, of course, Graham thought, she'd shaved the dog there.

Graham headed into the kitchen while asking if anyone else wanted anything. His women all said water, except Mrs Dunston, who said, 'If you could bring me a cup of coffee? With milk and sugar.'

'Ah, sure,' Graham said over his shoulder, wondering where this woman had left her hostessing skills. He passed a dog – presumably the past owner of all the hair on the sofa – as he walked into the kitchen. The dog, a medium-sized mixed breed, didn't move, open an eye or anything as Graham passed, which made Graham wonder if it was dead. He leaned down and put his hand on the dog's side, feeling for the rise and fall of breathing. The dog turned its head and stared at Graham through clouded eyes, his muzzle as gray as Graham's grandpa's hair. 'Good boy,' Graham said, petted the dog's head and scratched behind its ears. The dog sighed, closed its eyes, pressed for a second against Graham's hand then settled himself back on the cool tile floor. Graham figured that the family room was even too hot for the aging dog.

He poured the coffee, grabbed four bottles of water out of the fridge, found a tray sitting on the counter and put everything on it, including milk and sugar for his hostess, such as she was. He was obviously better at this than she was, he thought to himself.

'Ladies,' he said, coming into the family room.

'Now, isn't this pleasant?' Mrs Dunston said. 'Such a sweet boy.'

Graham took a seat next to Miranda on the loveseat that matched the sofa in all but dog hair, while his mother and Luna had both secured two of the easy chairs in the room. That left two unoccupied. He downed half the bottle of water in one gulp.

'Ma'am,' Luna said, 'we're here because there *was* an incident at U.T. but it didn't involve your son – directly. His friend, Bishop—'

'Ha! Friend! Use that word sparingly when talking about that you-know-what!' Mrs Dunston said.

'Yes, ma'am. The problem is, you see, Bishop Alexander was murdered Sunday night—'

'Murdered?' she exclaimed, sitting bolt upright on the sofa. 'And you think my Robert had something to do with it?'

'No, ma'am, not at all. We're just talking to anyone who had any problem with the victim, and I can certainly see that you did. Is your husband here, ma'am?'

Mrs Dunston was sputtering. Finally she said, 'You think I— My husband—' She stopped and took a breath. 'You're out of your mind!'

'Where can we find your husband?' Luna asked.

Mrs Dunston leaned back and crossed her arms over her abundant chest. 'Not a word!' she said. 'I'm not saying one word! You people! You come in here and accuse me—' She began sputtering again.

'No, ma'am,' Luna said, her tone soft. 'No one is accusing you of anything. I'm only interested in the incident that happened before winter break, when you went to pick up your son. I understand the victim was rather nasty?'

'Victim! Ha! My son was the victim! That no-good said things . . . I can't even repeat them, they were so vile!' She shook her head. 'He was a horrible boy! I can't say anyone deserves to be murdered, but, well, you know, maybe he did!'

'I'd like to speak to Mr Dunston as well, ma'am, if you could tell me where to find him?'

'Who are these other people?' the woman demanded, spreading her arms out to indicate Graham, Miranda and his mom.

'They're helping me with the case,' Luna said.

Pointing at Graham, she said, 'He's not old enough to be with the police! Neither is she!' Her finger moved to point at Miranda.

Graham stood up. 'Ma'am, I was Bishop Alexander's roommate—'

'Oh my God!' she screeched. 'You people, get out of here now!'

'Ma'am, please don't paint me with the same brush as Bishop! The guy was an asshole and I've been trying for two semesters to get moved somewhere else. I know he treated Bobby like crap. I've witnessed it. But he treated almost everybody like crap! Including, and maybe more so than anyone else, me.' Graham pointed at his mother. 'This is my mom, and this,' he said, his head indicating Miranda, 'is . . . ah . . . my girlfriend?'

Miranda nodded her head and smiled at Graham. Graham turned back to Mrs Dunston. 'My mom came in from out of town when this happened and she's been trying to clear my name. The Austin police think I killed him—'

'You hated him that much, too?' Mrs Dunston said.

'Well, yeah, pretty much. But the main reason is because he was killed – stabbed to death – in our room while I slept—'

'He'd been drugged!' Miranda threw in.

'Stabbed to death! My oh my. That's . . . well, it's just awful. Even if he did deserve it. How's Robert holding up?' she asked Graham.

'He's upset, needless to say—'

She sighed. 'Of course he is,' she said, shaking her head. 'I've never understood the hold that horrible boy had over my son.' She stopped and looked at Luna. 'That day when we went to pick up Robert for winter break – that wasn't the first time my husband and I saw him belittle our boy.'

Graham sat back down. Now, he thought, we're finally getting somewhere!

Mrs Dunston was like her house, I thought. Overdone and overwrought. My first inkling of her taste – or lack thereof – was walking between the Tara-like columns of the front porch and then hearing the chimes inside the house play 'Lara's Theme' from *Dr Zhivago*. I mean, Tara and Lara don't even rhyme. Yes, sometimes I can be a taste snob. Other times I'm just a bitch.

When she finally started to tell us about the many other times Bishop Alexander had abused Bobby Dunston in his parents' presence, her husband walked in the front door.

Bobby definitely took after his mother. Mr Dunston reminded me of the description of Ichabod Crane in 'The Legend of Sleepy Hollow.' Tall, skinny, anemic, an Adam's apple you could rest a coffee cup on and Coke-bottom bottle glasses. When he came in the front door, his wife lumbered up from her seat and called out, 'David! It's about time you got home! Come in here now!'

The hapless David came in and stared at us as a group, then individually. His wife said, 'Don't stand there gawking, for crying out loud! These people are with the Austin police! That horrible friend of Robert's has been *murdered*!' The woman couldn't hide the glee that came out with the word 'murdered.'

'Oh,' David Dunston said.

'Is that all you have to say? Robert could be next, for all we know!' his wife screamed at him.

'Really, that's not—' Luna started but was drowned out by Mrs Dunston.

'I told you he should have stayed home and gone to that Christian school! But, oh no, you had to have him go *there*, just because you went there! But you didn't even graduate, so I never under—'

Luna stood up. 'Mrs Dunston, please. You're getting off subject here—'

'This is *my* house!' the woman almost spat. 'You don't tell me what I can do in my house!'

'Missy, honey,' the hapless David said. 'Calm down, dear.'

'You shut up!' she said to her husband.

I had to wonder if we were ever going to get back to their past encounters with Bishop Alexander. So, to move things along, I said to the husband, 'Your wife was going to tell us about past incidents where Bishop Alexander was rude to Bobby in front of y'all. Other than the one before winter break.'

'Rude?' Missy – I couldn't imagine a more inappropriate name for this woman – Dunston said, still standing, arms akimbo, furrowed brow intact. '*Rude* isn't the word! David! Tell her the word!'

'Ah . . .' her husband started, but she cut off anything he might actually have said.

'Disgusting is one word! Inexcusable is another word! How about depraved? David, don't you think that's a good word?'

'Well, yes—'

'I think it's an apt word! Depraved! That's what he was!'

Luna, still standing, waved her hands downward. 'Shall we all sit for a while and calm down—'

'I'm calm! How dare you insinuate that I'm not calm!' Mrs Dunston shouted.

David moved to his wife and drew her down on the couch, her large bottom (yes, I'm a bitch) leaving no room for him to sit anywhere but on the dog-hairy throw.

'Could you tell me as well as you can remember the details of those other encounters?' Luna asked.

'I just can't!' Mrs Dunston said, fanning herself with her hand. I'd been thinking about doing the same thing since we walked into the room but felt it would be rude. Rudeness no longer seemed an issue.

'Mr Dunston?' Luna asked, looking at the husband.

'Well,' he started, then was silent for what seemed an eternity, although maybe less than a minute. 'Every time we saw him, ah, Bishop, he, ah, was saying mean things to Robert.'

'Such as?' Luna pressed.

He shrugged one very frail shoulder. 'Ah, well, he'd call him names.'

'In front of you?' Luna asked.

David Dunston nodded his head but said nothing.

'Names,' Luna said. 'Such as?'

'Ah, I don't know, you know, like stupid—'

'He called him a worthless piece of you-know-what!' Mrs Dunston supplied. 'And he said that if he didn't do what he – that horrible boy – told him to do then he'd regret it.'

'Uh-huh,' David Dunston agreed, nodding at his wife.

I was beginning to see that Bobby Dunston might have a physical resemblance to his mother, but his flunkiness he got wholeheartedly from his dad.

'Oh, he said so many horrible things, with David and I right there to hear them! I can only imagine what he said to Robert when we *weren't* there!'

'How many times did you witness these encounters?' Luna asked.

Missy Dunston looked to her husband. He shrugged. 'I'm not sure,' she said into the void. 'But they've been friends – if you want to call it that! – since last year. So several times, although he never actually came by to meet us or anything! We just saw him when he wanted something from Robert! Which seemed like always!'

Again, David Dunston nodded his agreement.

'And you found this more than unpleasant, I would assume,' Luna said.

'Oh, goodness, yes! I could have killed that—' Missy Dunston stopped and looked at her husband.

He turned from her and looked at Luna. 'That's just a, you know, expression.'

'What about you, Mr Dunston?' Luna asked. 'How did you feel about the way Bishop Alexander talked to your son?'

'Ah, well, ah, I, you know, didn't like it. Much.'

I was ready to leave. I didn't think Missy Dunston would go to the physical effort of doping my son and killing Bishop. I mean, the stabbing alone would wind her. And David – well, I'm sure he'd have to ask his wife's permission to kill a roach in the silverware drawer.

I gave Luna a look and a head nod toward the front of the house. She read me like a book. She stood up and said, 'I want to thank both of you for your time. You've been very generous. And, Mrs Dunston, thanks for the water. We should be heading back to Austin.'

'David, get me the phone!' Missy Dunston said. 'I have to call Robert now!'

'Honey, he may, you know, be in class?'

'Just *hand me the phone*! And see these people to the door!'

We all left as quickly as we could.

Graham was pretty sure his mom knew what he'd been up to in the bathroom of his dorm room. She had an eye for stuff like this. He noticed when he'd gone in the room with Bishop's mother that one of the cabinet doors underneath the sink had been left open. He'd glanced inside then and saw something that looked interesting. He wasn't able to grab it at the time because the mother wanted to go and he knew Champion was just outside the door. But when he'd gone back with his mom and Champion, he'd felt he had to find out what it was. It was a wad of paper stuck behind the back of the closed drawer. He'd got down on his hands and knees and carefully extracted it, sat on his butt on the floor and spread the paper out, pressing out the wrinkles. It was an economics test. He'd had no idea what that meant. He was pretty sure Bishop had an econ class last semester – he'd heard him bitching about the prof – but why would he hide it? Or had he? Had it just got stuck behind the drawer somehow? But that was Graham's drawer it was stuck behind. How had it got there? And why hadn't Graham noticed the drawer hadn't closed all the way? Mostly, he'd thought, because nothing much closed all the way in the dorm room – drawers, cupboards, closet doors. It was an old dorm. And he rarely cared about things like drawers shutting, etc. His mom could testify to that.

So, why was that test paper stuck behind his drawer? What did it signify? Then he'd decided he'd been in the john too long. That cop would come busting in any minute, so he'd got up off the floor, wadded the test paper back up and stuck it in his pocket. And gone back into the room to listen to his mom and the cop snipe at each other.

Now he sat in his motel room, looking at the paper he'd once again pressed out on his bed. It was still just an econ test. Miranda was in the bathroom of his motel room, and, coming out, she noticed the paper on the bed.

'What's that?' she asked.

Graham shrugged. 'Something I found in the bathroom back at the dorm,' he said.

She sat down on the bed and looked at it, turning it so that it faced her. 'It's an econ test,' she said.

'Yeah, duh. I sorta noticed that.'

'Where did it come from?'

'I just told you – the bathroom—'

'No,' Miranda said, 'I mean how did it get there?'

'I guess Bishop dropped it or something—'

'It's not graded,' she said.

'Huh?' Graham offered.

She pointed at the top of the page and turned the paper around to Graham. 'Look. No grade. And all the answers.'

'Yeah, so?'

'Jeez, I thought I was messing around with a bright boy. My mistake,' she said, as sarcastically as his mother, Graham thought. Maybe he should reconsider this relationship.

'You know,' he said, 'you're beginning to remind me of my mother.'

Miranda smiled. 'Thank you,' she said.

'I mean, you're just as sarcastic and know-it-all as she is!'

'Again, I say thank you. But let me point out what you seem to be ignoring here: this paper is not graded; this paper has all the answers on it. This paper is the prof's test. I'm guessing that somehow Bishop got hold of the test answers before taking the test. Am I getting through to you?'

'Can it, *Mom*,' Graham said. She just grinned in response. 'So Bishop was stealing test answers. This does not surprise me. He was pretty stupid – he'd have to cheat to pass anything.'

'Test answers are a big business, you know,' Miranda said.

'Yeah?'

'Yeah. I'm thinking this might have something to do with why somebody offed him.'

Graham looked at her, then down at the paper. 'You think we should go tell my mother and Luna about this?'

Miranda grabbed the paper, stood up and headed for the door. 'Ya think?'

THIRTEEN

When I came out of the bathroom, Graham and Miranda were sitting on Luna's bed, with Luna, and all three were staring at a piece of paper on the bed spread.

'What?' I said.

'We think we know why Bishop was killed!' Miranda said.

'Hush,' Luna said. 'There's another thread to pull, that's all.'

I got down on my knees by the bed to look at the paper. I would have preferred to sit on the bed but there was no room. I looked at it for a long moment, sighed, and said, 'OK, I don't get it.'

'It's an economics professor's test, with the answers. The one the prof or the T.A. keeps for grading purposes. See? The answers are all here in the same font as the test itself,' Miranda said.

'OK,' I said, still not fully understanding.

'Graham found it stuck behind the drawer in his dorm bathroom!' Miranda said.

Light dawned. OK, so my horny son wasn't going in there for condoms. Did I need to buy some for him? Should a mother do that? Did Miss Manners have an answer to that one?

'Where did you get it?' I asked. Graham hadn't taken economics yet and wasn't interested in taking it, as far as I knew.

'I think Bishop stuck it behind my drawer,' Graham said. 'That's the only thing I can think of.'

'And this is significant because?' I asked.

'Test answers are a big business on campus, y'all!' Miranda said, obviously getting a little miffed that no one found this as significant as she obviously did. 'And Gretchen Morley had something she wanted to give back to Tina Ng but Tina told her to keep it! Like maybe other tests?'

'We don't know that,' Luna the wet blanket said.

'It seems to fit,' I said, to which Miranda threw up a fist for me to bump. I did it, but grudgingly.

'Like I said,' Luna said, 'it's another thread to pull.'

'So maybe we should start pulling?' I suggested.

Luna sighed. 'You're not going to like what I have to say. Any of you. But,' she said and sighed again, 'we need to bring Champion in on this.'

She was right: none of us liked that one little bit.

Champion was sitting at his desk in his cubicle staring at his computer screen. He was thinking about maybe playing solitaire. It would get him just as far on the case as everything else he seemed to be doing. Not to mention he couldn't find the Pugh kid. Or Luna. Or the mom. He was thinking of getting the Texas Rangers on it, send them to Podunk wherever, the place where they came from. He only wished he could remember the name of the burg.

This whole thing was his wife's fault. His ex-wife. Since the divorce he couldn't concentrate. Or maybe it was since his source of nookie had dried up. He was obviously horny. Every woman he saw seemed to have a neon sign on her head that said, 'I've got one!'

Champion sighed. If it wasn't for his wife – ex-wife – he'd be able to concentrate on the case at hand. He had a kid murdered. A very unpopular kid. Maybe two people in the whole world liked the kid, and one of 'em wasn't even his own mother. But he wasn't really sure about Morley. She was mad at him but did that make her hate him? And Bobby what's-his-name. Could he really have liked that little scumbag with everything the vic said to and about him? So maybe nobody in the world, including his own mother, liked him. Champion was beginning to be pretty damn sure that, had he known the kid when he was alive, he too wouldn't have liked him. Hell, even dead he didn't like him very much.

Everybody had a motive. But only Graham Pugh had the opportunity. *If*, and that was a big if, he hadn't been roofied.

The bullpen was emptying out. He was almost the only one left. But then he didn't have anywhere to go like the rest of the department. He currently lived in a rented mobile home in a trailer park where he was pretty sure half the residents he'd arrested at one time or another also lived. He really didn't want to go there. And he didn't want to go to his favorite cop bar because, let's face it, some asshole would want to talk about the case. If he went to another bar and set the precedent of drinking alone, that could start a whole new problem. He'd seen his own father go down that road and it was paved with sorrows.

His best friend, another cop stationed out in the boonies, was married with kids and, although his friend kept telling him his wife herself had invited him out to dinner, Champion didn't really believe it. The wife was more a friend of Champion's wife than his.

Trying to clear his mind of extraneous bullshit, he decided maybe he should go by that motel where the Pughs and Luna were staying and stake it out. He'd already talked with the desk clerk and they hadn't checked out, and the kid's car was still parked in front of one of the rooms so they'd be coming back. He was sure of that. He decided to be there when they did.

We were still debating – OK, arguing – about whether or not to bring Champion in on what we'd found when there came a hearty knock on the door. Hearty being another word for aggressive. The four of us looked at each other, then at the door. There was another knock.

Then a voice. 'Luna, I know you're in there! You and the Pughs! Open up!'

'Well, I guess that ends the debate,' Luna said, standing and going to the door.

'No, it doesn't!' I whispered loudly.

She opened the door and Champion pushed into the room.

'Where's your warrant?' I demanded, standing up, hands on hips.

'Don't need one. Luna invited me in.'

'She did not—' I started but Luna interrupted.

'Yes, I did,' she said, and closed the door behind Champion.

'Shit,' I said in my most ladylike way and flopped down on the bed. I noticed my son was looking at the floor and

Miranda had her hand on his arm while shooting daggers with her eyes at either Luna or Champion – or probably both.

And so Luna told him what we'd been up to, leaving out the part about going to San Antonio, and showed him the test paper. And, of course, explained its possible dire meaning.

'So you're saying this Ng woman – whom I've met and can't imagine her big enough to stab anyone to death, not to mention a fully grown man – and Morley are running a test business, and what? Alexander wanted in?'

'Yes!' said Miranda, jumping up. 'Don't you see? Bishop would do anything for a buck, right? So this scam was perfect for him. He probably bought a test through Morley then figured why should she get the big bucks when he could get in on the score? So—'

'Does she always talk like that?' Champion asked, looking at Graham.

He shrugged. I noticed my son hadn't said a word since Champion came in the room. I wanted to take him in my arms and rest his head on my shoulder but knew that would be the last thing he'd want. He's a big boy, I kept telling myself. A grown man, sort of.

'Talk like what?' Miranda demanded. 'I'm just telling you the lay of the land—'

'You watch a lot of cop shows, don't you?' Champion asked.

'I'm serious!' she shouted.

Champion couldn't hide that awful, shit-eating grin of his as he said, 'I know that you are.'

'Who's your supervisor? I want your badge number!' Miranda shouted.

Luna walked over to her and encouraged her back on the bed next to Graham. 'He's just yanking your chain, honey,' Luna said.

'But this is serious!' Tears sprang up in Miranda's eyes, threatening to spill over. 'He wants to arrest Graham and he can't! He just can't!' At which point the threatening tears were no longer a threat – they were as real as the sobs that accompanied them.

Graham took her in his arms and held her. 'It's gonna be all right,' he cooed. 'I know it's gonna be all right.'

'Look, kid,' Champion said with a sigh, sitting down beside me on the bed and leaning his elbows on his knees as he stared across at my son. 'I'm beginning to get a hint that maybe you didn't do this. And I kinda hope that you didn't. But I have nothing to prove it. This test answer crap – is it for real?'

'Seems to be,' Graham said, while Miranda sat up to stare at Champion.

'So Ng and Morley and maybe others have this thing going selling test answers to the unwashed masses,' Champion said while Graham and Miranda nodded. 'And maybe the vic buys one from either his girlfriend or the Ng chick. How am I doing so far?'

'Very well,' Miranda said.

'OK, so, being the money-grubbing asshole that he is – excuse me, was – he tries to weasel his way into their scam.'

'Yes,' Miranda said.

'So why don't they share?' Champion asked. 'You say there's a lot of money in the racket.'

'Because,' Graham said, 'Bishop wouldn't want a share. He'd want the whole thing, or at least the lion's share of it. He was a greedy bastard.'

'So I'm beginning to see. Blackmailing his own mother.' Champion shook his head. 'Of course, she raised him so she probably got what she deserved.'

'So how do we prove any of this?' Luna, the pragmatist, threw in.

'First,' Champion said, 'we go for the weakest link.'

'Gretchen Morley!' we all said in unison.

Champion stood up. 'Y'all have to stay here. Me and Luna will take care of—'

'Not on your life!' Miranda said, jumping up.

'Sit!' Champion ordered.

'Hey, I'm not a dog, you know!'

'Do it anyway!' Champion said.

'You can't talk to me—' the girl started but Luna jumped in.

'Miranda,' Luna said, standing next to Champion, 'we have to do this by the book. If we find something, we need to keep a chain of evidence. If she spills her guts, we need to Mirandize her, and we can't have non-police personnel in the room. This could cause a conflict at trial – if it ever goes to trial.'

'Oh, it's going to trial!' Miranda said.

'From your lips to God's ears,' E.J. said. Graham looked at his mother, smiled a strained smile and said, 'Amen.'

'At least take Mrs Pugh!' Miranda said.

'We can't,' Luna assured her, keeping her voice calm.

Miranda flung herself on the bed next to the kid and said, 'This sucks!'

Champion moved to her and patted her on the head. 'It'll be OK.'

She shook his hand off. 'Woof, woof,' she said.

He grinned and he and Luna headed for the door.

Once in Champion's unmarked car, Luna said, 'So you're coming around, finally.'

'Don't start!' Champion said, fastening his seatbelt as he started the car. 'I'm still on the fence. I could fall to either side, you know.'

'You know Graham didn't do it. Your pride's just in the way.'

'Shit, woman, I have no pride. My ex got it in divorce,' he said.

Luna laughed. 'Nate, I really think you need to get laid.'

'Are you volunteering?' he asked, giving her a look.

'You know my husband would gut you like a chicken just for asking that, don't you?'

'Yeah. Don't mess with a guy who's done federal time, right?'

'Exactly,' Luna said.

'Duly noted,' Champion said and headed toward campus.

'What do we do now?' I asked Graham and Miranda.

Graham shrugged and Miranda looked dejected. After a few seconds, she brightened. 'I know!'

'What?' Graham said, obviously infected by her enthusiasm.

'We need to look into Tina Ng. I mean, really look into her—'

'How are we supposed to do that?' I asked.

'The computer,' Graham said. 'We need to find someone with mad computer skills—'

'We have someone,' Miranda said.

'Who?' Graham asked.

She grinned. 'My cousin, Dave.'

Graham frowned. 'Ah, Miranda, he's a nice enough guy and all but he's a serious stoner—'

'Yes, he is that, but he is also a computer whizz. He broke into the CIA's database when he was twelve. Instead of arresting him, they had him build them a new firewall. They haven't been hacked since.'

'But that was—'

'How do you think he affords that apartment?' Miranda asked.

'Dealing?' Graham suggested.

She shook her head. 'Nope. He's a gamer. You'd be surprised if I told you some of the games he's designed.'

'So you think he'd do this for us?' I asked. 'Check out Ng?'

'Absolutely,' Miranda said.

'Well, then, let's get out of here,' I said and headed for the door.

Graham pulled into the parking lot of Dave Wisher's fourplex. Miranda had called ahead to make sure Dave was available and, according to Miranda, of course he was. She explained that Dave did almost all of his classes online and seldom left his apartment. Groceries were delivered, his friends came to him and even his dope was delivered. He rarely needed to leave. The question was more was he straight enough to help rather than was he physically there?

The three of us climbed the stairs and Graham rapped on the door to the apartment. When it opened, the smell almost knocked me over. It had been long enough that I would probably get a contact high just walking in. I was sort of looking forward to it.

'Hey, Pugh! Cuz! Who's the hot chick?' he said. It took me a moment before I realized he was talking about me.

'Jeez, man!' Graham said, frowning. 'That's my mom!'

Miranda moved forward, pushing her cousin aside. We followed her, Graham closing the door behind him. 'Hey, ma'am, no disrespect meant!' Dave Wisher said, looking at me and grinning. 'But you're, you know, like, well, hot.'

'Wisher!' Graham said.

'Come on, Dave. Behave,' Miranda said. 'Like I said on the phone, this is some serious shit and we need your skills.'

'I got skills,' he said, and I could tell that, even as early as it was, Dave was stoned out of his gourd, as we used to say back in the day. But it was possible that he functioned best that way.

'Yeah, man, try to focus!' Graham said.

Dave looked at me again and grinned. 'I can't promise nothing, man.'

'Shit!' Graham said under his breath. 'Mom, you wanna, you know, take a hike?'

'Graham!' Miranda said. 'Dave will behave or I'll tell his mother.'

The grin escaped Dave Wisher's face. 'You wouldn't do that, would you, Cuz?'

'Not if you get down to business. We need a complete background check on somebody, including banking records.'

'I'm not supposed to do that,' Dave said, tap, tap, tapping away on his keyboard. 'If I get caught they'd have my nuts this time.'

'But you won't get caught, will you?' Miranda said.

'Shit, no. You got a name?'

'Tina Ng. That's spelled "n-g".'

Dave shook his head. 'Gotta have a vowel, man.'

'It's Vietnamese,' I said.

He smiled up at me and attempted to bat his eyelashes. I thought for a moment he'd fallen asleep. 'OK,' he said. 'I can dig it.'

He put in Ng's name, tapped some more and then said, 'Here's the stuff from the school.'

The three of us leaned over Dave's shoulder to read the information. Pretty generic stuff: name, address in Austin, permanent address in Palo Alto, California, phone numbers, and *voila*, a social security number.

'Okey-dokey,' Dave said. 'Here we go.' He hit some more keys, whistled a tune and pulled up her grades. 'Straight As. Graduated two years ago. In the graduate studies program for economics. T.A. Teaches some freshman and sophomore poli-sci classes and a couple of other things.'

'What other things? Economics, for instance?' Miranda asked.

He did some more tapping then said, 'Not this semester, but last semester, yeah. Took over for a T.A. Went into labor.'

'It says that there?' Miranda asked, leaning forward and frowning.

'Naw. I knew the chick. Kinda worried cause I banged her once, but this guy shows up and says it's his so I, you know, relaxed.'

'Congrats,' Graham said, only to get elbowed by both Miranda and myself.

'What?' he said, moving out of elbow range.

Miranda and I just looked at each other and rolled our eyes.

'So what about bank accounts?' I asked Dave.

'I'm looking!' Then he took his eyes off the screen for a second and looked up at me where I was leaning over him. 'You know, you can rest one of those on my shoulder if you'd like,' he said, eyeing my boobs.

Graham whacked him on the back of the head. 'Stop it! She's married! To my dad! You know, because she's *my mom*?'

'That hurt!' Dave said, turning back to face the screen. 'Bank records coming up.'

Gretchen Morley was in her room when Champion and Luna knocked on her door. On seeing them, she threw up her hands and said, 'O-M-G, not y'all again.'

'Really?' Luna asked, looking at Champion. 'I can't believe people actually say that in initials.'

Champion shrugged. 'I don't know about people but *she* certainly does.'

'*What* do you want *this* time?' Morley said, not moving from her doorway nor inviting them in.

'We need to talk about your testing scam,' Champion said. 'We can do it out here so all your, excuse the expression, *sisters* can hear, or we can come inside.'

Morley had gone pale at the mention of the testing scam and moved back into the room.

'I have no idea what you're talking about,' she said, turning her back on them.

'Yeah, well, I think you do,' Champion said. 'I think you know exactly what I'm talking about and I think it's about time you spilled your guts. So to speak.'

Gretchen Morley turned to face them, some color back in her cheeks and a stern look on her face. 'I'm calling my attorney and I'm not saying another word.'

With that, she grabbed her cell phone and dialed.

Tina Ng's banking records showed monthly deposits of four hundred and fifty dollars for the past two years. 'T.A. salary. Really sucks, huh?' Dave said.

'Anything else?' I asked.

He tap, tap, tapped some more then said, 'Couple of checks for a hundred here and a hundred there.' He looked up at me and batted his eyes again. 'Parents, you think?'

'Maybe,' I said. 'You'd think she'd be getting more for a cheating scam.'

'Wait, now,' Dave said. 'Here's a monthly debit to the bank.' He left that screen, went to another then back to Ng's bank records. 'Yeah. What I thought. It's the fee for a safe deposit box.'

I sat down on the nearest beanbag chair and Miranda plopped down next to me. 'So that's it?' she said. 'No way we can get into her safe deposit box, right?'

I shook my head. 'We'd need a search warrant, which we can only get through Champion, and I doubt if there's enough evidence at this point for any judge to sign off on it. If, and it's a big if, Champion would even listen to what we've got.'

Dave had turned from his screen to look at us. Well, me. I was being modest. 'Sorry, Pugh's mom. Anything else I can do?' He brightened. 'Back rub?'

'Just a minute,' I said and pulled my notepad and a pen out of my purse. I began writing a list of names – Gretchen, Ng, Bishop Alexander, Gaylord Fuchs, Bobby Dunston and his parents, Bishop's mom and Lexie Thurgood. I tore off the sheet from my notepad and handed it to Dave. 'This is a long shot, I know, but can you just run these names and see if there are any connections?' I shrugged. 'That's all I've got at this point.'

'Sure,' Dave said. 'For you, anything.'

I laughed, got up awkwardly from the beanbag chair and patted Dave on the head. 'You're good for a middle-aged woman's ego, you know that, Dave?' I said, and Graham, Miranda and I left.

'You're really just going to sit there?' Luna asked.

'My attorney is on her way,' Morley said. 'Until then, I'm saying squat.'

'It's her right,' Champion said. 'I mean, so what if it seals the deal. It's her right.'

Morley's brow furrowed. 'What deal?'

'I don't have to answer you any more than you have to answer me,' Champion said.

'What deal?' she repeated.

'Oh,' Luna said. 'You mean because this definitely makes her suspect number one in her boyfriend – I mean *ex*-boyfriend's murder?'

'Hush now,' Champion said.

'Sorry,' Luna said. 'I guess I shouldn't have let the cat out of the bag.'

Champion sighed. 'Too late now. We'll just wait for her attorney to get here, then read her rights to her and cuff her. That should work.'

'Wait a minute! Wait a minute!' Morley said, panic in her voice. 'I didn't kill Bish! I swear! I loved him!'

Luna looked at Champion, shrugged and said, 'Remember that old song? "You only hurt the one you love"? Something like that.'

'Yeah, I remember. Don't make music like that anymore.'

'I know,' Luna said. 'The big-hair eighties was the death of it.'

'Don't I know it,' Champion said.

'No, now, y'all wait!' Morley said. 'I don't care what that song says! I didn't kill Bish! I didn't!'

And for the first time in her presence, Champion thought he detected traces of real tears in her eyes.

'We're not supposed to talk about it,' he said.

'But I didn't! I had no idea what she was going to do, I

swear it!' Morley said, real tears flowing down her peaches-and-cream cheeks.

Champion prided himself on the fact that he didn't yell 'Eureka!' or even point a finger and say 'Ah ha!' He simply said, 'Who?' in a quiet voice.

'Ah, I can't, I mean, oh, God. She'll kill me too! Oh, shit!' Morley said and began to sob. It wasn't the quietly controlled sobs he'd heard from her earlier when she was supposedly bemoaning the death of Bishop Alexander. No, these sobs were gut-wrenching, eye-swelling, face-blotching authentic sobs.

'No one's going to get near you,' Luna said. 'We'll take you into protective custody and you'll be safe.'

'You mean jail, don't you? You're going to take me to jail!' The sobs began to border on hysteria.

There was a knock on the door. Luna went to answer it. A woman stood before her. She looked fiftyish, fit and pissed off when she looked behind Luna and saw her client in hysterics.

'You two,' she said, 'out of here, now! I want to see my client.'

Champion and Luna stood up and left the room.

'What was on that list?' Miranda asked from the back seat of Graham's car.

'Just a list of the names of anybody associated with this.' I shook my head. 'I couldn't think of anything else we could get Dave to do. I mean, as far as computers go, I can turn them on and turn them off. Oh, yeah, and I can check my email.'

'Graham!' Miranda said, hitting my son on the back of his head, not a good thing to do when he's driving but I let it go. 'You've really let your mother down! Why haven't you taught her how to use the computer?'

'Because she wouldn't let me! And stop hitting me. It hurts!'

It was true. I'm a writer. I write books. Romance novels. And I believe in libraries. Library science was my minor in college. And I'd had plans to continue on to get a second degree in it but Willis sort of got in my way. So I ended up with only one degree, in English literature, which was my major. A BA in English lit and five dollars still won't get you a cup of coffee these days. So, this trip down memory lane is to explain why I don't Google or Goggle or whatever people do instead of going to a perfectly good library wherein you can find the wonders of the world in actual book form.

'Can either of you think of something we should have asked Dave to do?' I asked.

There was a minute of silence, then, from the back seat, 'No, I guess not.'

'Me neither,' said Graham.

'So why don't we go talk to Tina Ng? Let's just ask her what she has in her safe deposit box!' Miranda said.

'I don't think so,' I said. 'We don't want her alerted to what we're doing just yet. Besides, she doesn't say much when we're *not* accusing her of dastardly deeds. I can only imagine how closed mouth she'd be if we did.'

Miranda sighed. 'Yeah, you're probably right. I'm just so *frustrated*!'

'Aren't we all,' I said.

'Why don't y'all trade recipes on the cake you're gonna make me with the file inside? I think I'm going to need it,' my son said, heading his Toyota toward our motel.

'She's gotta be talking about Ng!' Luna said as she and Champion stopped on the drag for a cup of coffee.

'Definitely, and maybe if she tells her lawyer the truth, Nancy will be able to get her to 'fess up, for a deal, of course.'

'Nancy?' Luna asked as they sat down at a small table with their drinks.

'Nancy Richards. Morley's attorney. Known her for years. A real mover and shaker in Austin. Used to be a state senator.'

Luna sighed. 'Leave it to Morley to have a big gun.'

'Big gun or not, Nancy's no slouch. She'll see that it's gonna be in Morley's best interest to push Ng under the bus.'

Looking out the big plate-glass window by their table, Luna said, 'Now that's an odd couple.'

Champion looked out. 'Isn't that Gaylord Fuchs? Or Gay Fucks as the vic was so fond of calling him.'

'Yeah, you're right. But is that his wife?'

The two cops stared out the window at the little man and the not-so-little woman walking with him. She was several feet taller and at least one hundred and fifty if not two hundred pounds heavier. When they stopped to look in a store window, the woman leaned down and kissed Fuchs on the lips.

'Unless he's messing around, yeah, I'd say that's his wife,' Champion said.

'Now wait a minute!' Luna said. 'Lexie Thurgood so intimidated the vic that he had to put her down whenever he got the chance, and she was slightly taller than him. That woman, I'd say, is taller, too, but she'd also outweigh him by a lot, and I dare say she could have handled him with no help from her husband when Bishop made a pass. *If* he made a pass.'

'What do you mean *if*?' Champion said.

'I mean, I just can't see the misogynistic asshole that was Bishop Alexander coming on to a woman who looks like Mrs Fuchs. I mean, look at Gretchen Morley. She's a Barbie doll. Mrs Fuchs is more like Xena Warrior Princess.'

'A really big Xena Warrior Princess,' Champion said.

'Hey, look, I'm a big woman,' Luna said. 'And I know how guys like Alexander react to women like me, like Mrs Fuchs. They all want a Barbie doll. Not Xena. Or even Wonder Woman.'

'You think you're Wonder Woman?' Champion said with a raised eyebrow.

'You'll never know,' Luna said.

'OK, so what you're saying is maybe Fuchs lied?' Champion asked.

'Well, I dunno. Maybe?'

'So maybe we should have a chat with Mrs Fuchs?' Champion asked.

'Sounds like a plan,' Luna said.

We'd barely made it back to the motel before the rain came. It can come quickly in Central Texas, out of a seemingly clear blue sky, especially in winter. But this day had been overcast and threatening so the rain came as no real surprise. The surprise was the rapid dip in temperature. It had been in the mid-to-low fifties for the past few days but by the time we reached the motel it had dropped down to the thirties. Once inside my room, we turned the TV to the Weather Channel to find out what was going on. It wasn't going to be pretty. Ninety percent chance that the rain would turn to sleet by early evening, and the temperature was predicted to drop into the twenties by midnight. Icy roads were predicted for the next day.

'Well, at least I wasn't planning on leaving for home tomorrow,' I said.

'Or anytime in the near future,' said my dejected son, who was lying face down on Luna's bed.

'I'm not sure I'm ready for sleet and ice,' I said. 'Didn't bring any boots or scarves or gloves.'

'I have an extra pair of all-weather boots,' Miranda offered.

I looked down at her obvious size six feet, then down at my size tens. 'Thanks, but—'

'I have a scarf and some extra gloves, though,' she said.

I smiled. 'Thanks. The scarf might fit.'

'Jeez, Mother! You can just go buy—' started my son, but was interrupted by hoots from both Miranda and myself.

'When freezing conditions have been announced?' Miranda said. 'As of the moment it began raining every store in Austin was sold out of anything warm. Doubt if you could find a windbreaker left anywhere.'

'Oh, come on—' he started.

'And umbrellas. I think people in this area think of umbrellas as disposable. Because every time it rains they have to go out and buy a new one,' I said. 'And they're all gone within fifteen minutes!'

'Ain't it the truth!' Miranda said. 'I have an extra one of those, too, if you need it.'

'Thanks, but I have one in my car—' I stopped myself. 'Yeah, I might need it, seeing as my car's not here.'

We were interrupted from this titillating discussion of the shortcomings of the buyers for every retail shop in Austin by the ringing of Miranda's phone. She picked it up, looked briefly at the screen and said, 'Hey, Dave. What's up?'

The slight frown on her face turned into a tentative smile, one that grew as she listened. Then she said, 'We're on our way!'

*   *   *

'We shouldn't go talk to her now,' Luna said, frowning at Champion. 'With her husband right there.'

'Why not? See how she takes the news?'

'The news?'

'You know, that Bishop Alexander came on to her. She might not be aware of it.'

'You have a point.'

They left their drinks on the table – although it was a self-bussing establishment – and headed out the door.

'Damn!' Luna said, pulling the collar of her winter jacket up to cover her ears. 'When did it get so cold?'

'And start raining?' Champion asked, sticking his hand out from under the coffee shop's awning.

'Shit, they're heading somewhere fast!' Luna said, spying the Fuchses as they dashed off.

'See where they go. Probably trying to get out of the rain,' Champion said.

'You sure they didn't see us?' Luna asked as she hurried along the sidewalk, her head bent to keep from getting soaked. It wasn't working.

'So what if they did?' Champion said, walking fast, hunched over from the rain that was fast becoming sleet. 'We're just following a really weak hunch. And they have no idea what we're doing.'

'They went in that store,' she said, pointing at a high-end kitchen store. 'I love this place.'

'Remember, we're not here to shop!' Champion said.

'Actually, that's what we should be doing! Just a coincidence we ran into them?'

Champion shrugged. 'Could work. What are we looking for?'

'Specifically?' Luna asked and laughed. 'One does not come into a place like this for a pair of kitchen scissors. One comes into a place like this to see all the things one wishes one could afford.'

'Oh, does one?'

'Don't make fun.'

'Why not?'

They entered the store, Luna unable to take her eyes of the wares. Hundred-dollar – each – knives; butcher-block cutting boards made of wood Luna was pretty sure was endangered; things that sliced, diced and julienned; other things that graded in five different degrees; juicers that could handle up to twelve oranges at a time; blenders with more buttons than her car; food processors, the cost of which would pay half her monthly mortgage; and so many wondrous things that Luna was afraid she was going to hyperventilate. She was thinking that she'd absolutely have to bring Pugh here when Champion touched her on the shoulder.

'There they are,' he whispered, pointing to a section of the store that had obviously been an add-on. There was a small ramp leading to an open space big enough for a single door that led to another room.

'Ooo!' Luna said, spying not the Fuchses but the incredible array of tablecloths, napkins, placemats and other textiles.

'Get a grip!' Champion said, taking her by the arm and leading her up the ramp.

'This one!' Luna said, grabbing a tablecloth covered in Santa and his reindeer that sat upon a table marked clearance.

'Christmas is over!' Champion said, hoping Luna was just putting on a show to make the Fuchses think that he and Luna were unaware of their presence.

'Jeez, Champion! Christmas comes every year, you know? And this is a pretty good price.'

'You're kidding, right?' he whispered, moving close to her ear.

'Just play along, dumbass.'

'Don't call me dumbass.'

'Don't act like one.'

'How about this one?' Champion said, pointing at a table-cloth adorned with poinsettias.

'A little loud,' Luna said.

'And Santa and a dozen reindeer aren't loud?'

'Only when they're on the roof.'

'Oh, you're funny.'

'Thank you.'

'Well, hello!' came another voice.

Looking down, Champion saw Gaylord Fuchs standing before him.

'Hey, Mr Fuchs!' Champion said. 'How ya doing?'

'Just great. Detective Luna, right?'

'You remembered!' she said, reaching down to shake his hand.

'Just because I'm short doesn't mean my memory is,' Fuchs said.

'Ignore him, he teases,' said the woman standing behind him.

'Sorry, this is my wife, Annabelle. Annabelle, these are the detectives looking into that murder on campus.'

She held out her hand, frowning. 'Awful, just awful!' she said. 'It's usually such a safe campus! I can't believe such a thing happened.'

'I know,' Luna said, shaking her head. 'You just never know! It must have been quite a weird feeling after what he did to you.'

Annabelle Fuchs frowned. 'Pardon? After who did what to me?'

'The victim, Bishop Alexander. After the way he abused you—'

Annabelle Fuchs looked from Luna to her husband. 'Honey?' she said.

'Ah, he was at one of our parties,' Fuchs said in a rush. 'He acted like an idiot.'

His wife laughed. 'So many of them do! But I'm not sure which one he was,' she said, smiling at Luna. 'Sorry.'

'Well, as long as there was no real harm done,' Luna said, smiling back.

'You're looking at the clearance items, I see,' Annabelle said. 'They really discount this stuff like crazy. Makes you wonder how big their markup is in the first place.'

'No kidding,' Luna said. 'But I'll tell you this: if I ever win the lottery, this is where most of the money will go!'

Annabelle laughed. 'I hear you!'

'If you're gonna buy it, let's do it,' Champion said. 'I was due back at the station thirty minutes ago!'

'Jeez, you're always in such a rush,' Luna said, putting the tablecloth down. 'I'm going to have to think about it,' she said, then said goodbye to the Fuchses and the two headed out the door.

*   *   *

It was a mess trying to get back to Dave Wisher's apartment. People in Central Texas don't have snow tires, chains or other cold weather gear to deal with sleet and icy streets. We just slip and slide and bump into each other instead. There was one very slow head-on collision we witnessed on the slow-moving Lamar Blvd., a car mating with a lamp pole and another on the sidewalk, only inches away from an establishment with a large plate-glass window. We weaved our way around all this and made it to Dave's apartment in just under half an hour. Earlier we'd made the same trip in ten minutes.

Dave opened the door with a bong to his lips. He coughed uncontrollably as he allowed us in and pointed to the beanbag chairs. When the coughing finally subsided, he took a deep breath, grinned and said, 'Smooth shit!'

'Tell them!' Miranda said, having refused to tell us herself the contents of the telephone call from her cousin.

'Huh?' was Dave's response.

'What you told me on the phone! Jeez, how stoned are you?' she demanded.

'Not half as stoned as I plan on getting,' he responded. 'What did I tell you on the phone?'

'About what you found out when you did a comparison on the list of people E.J. gave you!' Miranda said.

Dave frowned. 'Who's E.J.?' I raised my hand. He looked at me and grinned. 'Oh, yeah, the hot mama!' The grin left his face and he looked at my son, his hands held up in a pleading manner. 'Don't hit me!'

Graham sighed. 'I'm not going to hit you, Dave. What did you find out?'

'About what?' Dave asked, the frown deepening.

I got up off the beanbag chair and went to stand next to Dave where he sat on a rolling chair in front of his computer. 'Remember I gave you that list of names? And you were going to check and see if there was any connection between any of them? I think you found something,' I said, smiling at him. 'That's why you called Miranda.'

'Oh, yeah! Right!' He grinned at me. 'I did!'

He stopped talking for a moment and I asked, 'And? What did you find?'

'Oh, you want me to tell you?'

'Please,' I said.

He nodded several times, turned to the computer and almost instantly the stoner was gone and the computer hack was in place. 'OK, see, I ran the names in a couple of algorithms and finally found some similarities. Like that chick with the two-letter no-vowel name?'

'Tina Ng,' I supplied.

'Yeah, her. Her student adviser for her undergraduate studies was one of the others on the list, that Fuchs guy. And also, another connection with those two, he recommended her for the T.A. program.' He looked up at me with puppy dog eyes. 'Does that help you?'

I looked over at Miranda and Graham, who were both standing now with faces showing varying degrees of surprise and/or elation.

Looking back at Dave, I asked, 'Any other connection? To any of the others?'

'Yeah, well, Fuchs was that guy Alexander's student adviser, too.'

'What about Gretchen Morley?'

'Huh?'

'Is Fuchs her student adviser?' I asked.

He looked back at the screen, tapped some keys then said, 'Uh-uh. Some chick, Reba Dailey, is her adviser,' he said.

'Bobby Dunston?'

Again with the taps. 'Nah. He and that Thurgood chick have the same adviser – Larry something Polish, I think.'

I looked at the name he pointed to. Maybe not Polish but definitely middle-European. I didn't even try to pronounce it.

'Nothing that ties the mother to anyone else?'

He shook his head. '*Nada*,' he said. 'But I did find something else.'

When he didn't elaborate, I asked, 'And what was that?'

'That chick with the two-letter name—'

'Tina Ng,' I supplied.

'Yeah, her. She's got another address different to the one the uni has for her.'

I turned and looked at Graham and Miranda, then turned back to Dave. 'Really? And what would that address be?'

'It's over off Enfield,' he said. And gave me the address.

I kissed the top of his head and he beamed up at me. 'We're engaged now, right?' he said.

'Absolutely,' I said and headed for the door, assuming Graham and Miranda would follow.

'So where the hell are they?' Champion demanded, standing in the empty motel room Luna shared with the Pugh woman.

'Hum, well—'

'Maybe they're in the kid's room.'

'You knocked fairly loud,' Luna advised him.

'Yeah, well, maybe they're hiding,' Champion said.

'You want to knock again?'

'No! I'm gonna get the manager to open the door!'

'You got a warrant?' Luna asked.

He raised an eyebrow. 'If the manager gives his OK I don't need no stinking warrant. The room doesn't *belong* to the kid, you know.'

Luna sighed. 'Whatever,' she said and sat down on her bed.

'You're not coming with me?'

'I think you can handle this all on your own.'

'You know where they are, don't you?' Champion demanded.

'No!' Luna said with a steady stare. 'I have no idea. And I'd tell you if I did. But, knowing Pugh, they could be anywhere.'

Champion made a sound like a sick moose and left the room.

As soon as the door closed behind him, Luna dialed Pugh's number – again. This time she heard the ringing, right there in the motel room. Noting the crumpled bedclothes on Pugh's bed, she rummaged around until she found the phone. She wondered, momentarily, if Pugh had done that on purpose, then decided it wasn't her style. If she wanted to ignore Luna she'd just not answer the call. Then, for another fleeting moment, she wondered if possibly Pugh had been kidnapped . . . One of the only possible reasons she could think of for Pugh to leave her phone behind.

But these thoughts were cut short when the door to the motel room opened and Pugh and the kids came bounding in.

'Boy, have we got information for you!' Graham's new girlfriend said, almost jumping up and down in her excitement.

Luna noticed Pugh put a hand on the girl's arm, restraining her.

'What's up?' Pugh asked Luna.

'Nothing much,' Luna responded. 'What's up with you?'

'Same. Nothing much.'

The two women stared at each other for a long moment until a sharp banging began on the door to their room. All eyes turned to Pugh.

'Champion?' she asked, looking at Luna.

'Nobody knocks like that but a cop,' Luna responded.

'Should we let him in?' Pugh asked.

Luna shrugged. 'What could it hurt?'

'Me!' Graham said.

Luna stood and ruffled his hair, an affectionate action she'd been doing since he was seven years old. 'You're almost off the hook,' she said and went to the door to let in a rather angry cop.

He was sputtering, he was so mad. I tried not to laugh but it was hard. We knew who'd done it and my son was going to be scot-free in seconds. As soon as Champion allowed us to speak.

He finally took a breath and I said, 'We know who did it—'

'Gaylord Fuchs,' Champion and Luna said in unison.

'Well, shit!' Miranda said and flopped down on a bed. 'How'd y'all find out?'

'You first!' Champion demanded.

'Fuchs was Tina Ng's student adviser during her undergrad days, and he's the one who recommended her for the T.A. position,' I said. 'Now you!'

Champion clammed up so Luna took on the tale. 'We saw Fuchs and his wife at that expensive kitchen store—'

'Oh, yeah! The one on the drag? I want to hit that before we leave—'

'Absolutely!' Luna said. 'My God, the shit they have in there—'

'Oh, for God's sake!' Champion said. 'The point of this is that Mrs Fuchs knew absolutely nothing about Bishop Alexander, or him reportedly groping her. Not to mention that she was definitely not his type.'

'So does any of this prove anything? And what are we saying happened?' I asked.

Champion sank down on the bed. 'No proof, to speak of. It's all circumstantial. What we need is a confession—'

'Which is why y'all went to Gretchen Morley's, right?' Miranda demanded. 'What happened?'

'She lawyered up,' Luna said.

'But I know her attorney,' Champion said, 'and I'm hoping she'll talk Morley into throwing at least Ng under the bus.'

'Do you think Morley even knows about Fuchs?' I asked.

'It could go either way,' Champion said. 'But, if I were Fuchs, I'd want as few people as possible knowing my involvement. I'd lay money on the fact that only Ng knows about him.'

'So if Morley throws Ng under the bus, so to speak,' I said, 'then you're hoping Ng in turn will do the same with Fuchs?'

Champion sighed. 'It's what we have.'

'Well,' I said, 'maybe we should push matters along ourselves.'

'Oh, shit,' Luna said. 'Pugh's got an idea. We're all in trouble now.'

There was no way this was going to work, Champion thought as he watched Miranda Wisher walk up the steps to Tina Ng's house. This wasn't the place near campus that was on her university papers, the one Luna and Pugh had been in earlier. No, this one was off Enfield, a section of the upper crust near the downtown area where some mansions had been turned into student housing and others stayed just the way God intended them. Tina Ng's house was neither a mansion or a used-to-be mansion. It was a rather modest home on a small lot that Champion knew would go for over half a million in that area. Maybe closer to three-quarters of a million. According to Pugh, the records showed Tina Ng owned the house outright, which meant she had heavy money coming in from somewhere.

They were all in the Pugh kid's beat-up Toyota, as it was less conspicuous than any other vehicle at their disposal. The mom had the front seat with Luna and Champion in the back. There was a little more leg room now that the Wisher girl was out of the car. The girl had insisted she be wired but, seeing as how she had a perfectly good cell phone that could pick up any conversation going on between herself and Ng, he had declined to wire her up. She was obviously disappointed but went in with her cell phone in her pocket nonetheless.

They could hear the chime of the doorbell when Wisher rang it, coming in loud and clear from the Pugh kid's phone. They saw and could also hear the front door of Tina Ng's home open.

And of course Tina Ng said nothing, just stared at Wisher. Finally Miranda said, 'Nice house.'

There was no response from Ng.

'Not the same one the police met you at earlier. So you live in two places, huh?'

Still no response.

Miranda said, 'We need to talk. May I come inside?'

'No,' Ng answered.

'OK, fine. Then I'll just go to the police with what I know,' Miranda said, which had not been part of the script Champion and Luna had laid out for the girl. Champion looked at Luna and glared.

'What?' Luna demanded, in a whisper. 'I had nothing to do with that!'

'Whatever,' Champion said and turned back to looking at the front door of Ng's house.

'. . . Nothing,' was all Champion heard when he turned his attention back to the conversation coming from the phone.

'What?' he whispered to the mom.

'If you two would stop talking, maybe we'll find out!' she fairly hissed back.

'Look—' Champion started, but he stopped when he heard Miranda Wisher speaking again.

'You have no idea what I know. Let's just say I'm real good at math and I can put two and two together in a nanosecond.'

Not a word from Ng.

'Fine. I can say what I have to say here on the porch for the whole world to hear, or just head on to the police station.'

'Where's your car?' Ng asked.

There was a pause before Miranda said, 'I walked.'

No reply from Ng.

'OK, fine!' Miranda said, turning her back on Ng. 'The next voice you hear will be a cop's.'

'Come in,' Ng said, and Champion could see that she'd turned her back and walked further into her home, leaving the door open. They could see Miranda follow her inside, shutting the door behind her.

'Y'all, I'm not real crazy about this—' Graham said, but stopped when he heard the girl's voice.

'Nice place,' Miranda said. 'You've got good taste.'

No response.

'Hey, is that an original Claudette? I took a semester of art history.'

'No.'

'You sure? Really looks like an original. You and Morley must be raking it in for you to have a place like this and such nice stuff,' Miranda said.

'I don't know what you're talking about,' Ng said.

'Oh, yeah, you do. And I want in.'

'In what?' Ng said.

'Your testing scam, of course.'

'I don't know what you're talking about,' Ng said.

Champion couldn't help but think this was probably the most Tina Ng had spoken within his hearing. She was obviously getting scared. *Bring it home, kid*, he thought.

'So here's the deal. Fifty percent or I go to the cops. That's fifty percent total. Whatever split you have with Morley comes out of your half.'

'You need to leave,' Ng said.

'Or what? You got a knife handy?' Miranda said.

'Oh, shit!' Graham said. 'Y'all get in there! She's gonna kill her!'

'Shut up!' Champion demanded, straining to hear Ng's response.

'Maybe,' was what he heard.

'OK, so it was you who did in old Bishop, huh? We sorta fig—'

'We?' demanded Ng.

'Me. I said me.'

'No, you didn't!' Ng shouted.

'Ow!' Miranda said, at which Graham bailed from the car with his phone, so any further discussion between the two young women was lost on Champion. So he decided he might as well follow the Pugh kid.

The door had obviously not locked behind Miranda when she followed Tina Ng inside, as Graham and Champion had no problem pushing their way in. Luna and I were only seconds behind. Ng had her arm around Miranda's neck in a chokehold. Miranda was at least five inches taller than Ng, but the tiny Vietnamese woman had Miranda's feet off the ground and Graham's new girlfriend's face was turning an ugly shade of purple. Champion grabbed Ng, pulling her to the ground while Graham caught Miranda in his arms. Meanwhile, while lying on the hardwood floor of her beautifully furnished home, Tina Ng managed to take Champion's feet out from under him, throwing him to the floor and then jumping on top of him, pounding him mainly in his manly regions. Or should I say formerly manly regions?

Luna got to Ng before she totally castrated Champion and pulled her off, although the five foot, eleven inch, two hundred pound Luna seemed to have to strain to do it. She got Ng pinned to the floor and cuffed her hands behind her back as I ran up to Champion to try to help him up.

'Don't touch me!' he said, lying on his back.

'You OK?' I asked.

'No,' he said.

'Do you want an ambulance?' I asked.

'And have every employee in the city – from the chief of police to the dog catcher – find out I got taken out by a ninety pound girl? No, I don't think so.'

I sat down on the floor next to him. 'I think it was some form of martial arts.'

'Ya think?'

'How long do you want to lie here?' I asked.

'As long as it takes,' he said. His eyes were closed, his face pointed at the ceiling, his knees up and his hands covering his gonads.

I felt a hand on my arm. 'Mom, let him alone. You take care of Miranda.'

'Does she need an ambulance?' I asked.

'Already called one,' Graham said.

'Have her meet them outside,' Champion said. 'Don't let them in here.'

'Right,' I said, getting to my feet.

'Really, Mom. It's not funny. Don't let them in.'

'Jeez, I won't. God, you men,' I said.

As I was heading toward Miranda, I heard Champion say, 'Thanks, kid.'

Miranda's normal color was coming back but the skin of her neck was definitely bruised – red now, but already turning darker – and she seemed to be fighting somewhat for breath.

'Come on,' I said, helping her to a standing position. 'Let's get you outside. I hear the sirens now.'

She nodded her head and took my arm as I led her out of Ng's house.

Champion ended up in the hospital after all. Ng had managed to dislocate one of his testicles and he was probably going to have to have an operation to fix it. Nobody at the cop shop was teasing him about it. As a matter of fact, according to Luna, every male employee at the jail was treating Tina Ng *very* carefully. Miranda was treated and released and Luna, Graham and I took her back with us to the motel.

'Is Ng talking?' I asked Luna as we all sat down on the beds of the room I shared with her.

'Not a word. But I sorta expected that,' Luna said.

'She appears to be verbally challenged,' I agreed.

'She's a bitch!' Miranda said, or croaked. Her voice hadn't come all the way back yet.

'You need to be a little less talky yourself,' I said. 'You need to let your throat heal.'

'She's still a bitch,' she whispered. Graham pulled her to him in a hug and she rested her head on his shoulder. I was going to have to stop wincing every time I saw this kind of thing with my son.

'I'll grant you that,' Luna said. 'But that doesn't get us any further with Gay Fucks.'

'Are you sure he's involved in this?' Graham asked. 'I mean, he's a nice guy. I know a few people who've had him as a counselor and they say he's really good.'

'Ever been to his house?' Luna asked.

'No,' Graham answered. 'Why?'

'Just wondering. Ng was definitely living above her reported means. I wonder if Fuchs' lifestyle will say the same thing.'

'Call Dave,' I said.

Miranda reached for her phone but Graham stopped her. 'I'll do it. Rest your voice. He's on speed dial?'

She nodded and punched in the number, putting the phone on speaker.

'Dave!' came the happy voice on the other end of the line.

'Hey, Dave, it's Graham Pugh—'

'Hey, Pugh! Man, how's that hot mama of yours?'

I grinned. 'Just fine, Dave!' I said. 'How are you?'

'Real good now that I hear your voice, sweet cheeks!'

Graham gave me a stern look. 'Never mind that crap. Dave, we need you to look up an address for us.'

'Like you don't have a phone book?'

We all looked at each other, then around the room. Sure enough, there was a phone book on a shelf under the nightstand where the actual landline was located.

'Just a minute, Dave!' I said as I grabbed the book.

'Mama, I'll wait a lifetime for you!'

'Can it, Dave, I mean it!' Graham said.

Luna, with a confused look on her face, said, 'Who's Dave and why does he have the hots for E.J.?' Turning to me, she said, 'Pugh, are you stepping out on Willis? 'Cause I'll tell!'

'God, no!' Graham almost shouted.

There was no listing for Gaylord Fuchs in the phone book. Since more and more people were foregoing landlines and just using cell phones, it wasn't surprising. Who knew when the phone company would start listing cell numbers? Maybe that was something we didn't want out there. I wasn't sure.

'No listing in the phone book,' I called out to Dave.

'OK, so give me the name and I'll do it the modern way.'

Graham gave him the name and spelled it.

'Oh, yeah. I remember this Fucks guy. You had me look him up earlier,' Dave said.

'That's Fuchs, Dave. A long "u",' I said.

'No shit? Looks like fucks to me.'

'Yeah, it does,' I agreed.

'Just find the damn thing!' Graham said.

'Jeez, Pugh, why you getting so uptight?' Dave asked, but I could hear his fingers on the keyboard and knew he was doing his thing. 'Yeah, here it is. On Avenue H.' And he gave us the number.

'Thank you, Dave,' I said.

'For you, darlin', anything.'

'I'm hanging up,' Graham said and did so. Turning to me, he said, 'Mother, you are encouraging him!'

'Yes, I certainly am,' I agreed with a big smile.

Without further ado we hopped into Luna's SUV and headed to Avenue H. It was within walking distance of the campus and proved to be an old Victorian, not unlike our attorney Stuart Freeman's office. It was also in as good a shape as Stuart's. It was painted a grayish blue with white shutters and trim, and was surrounded by more than its fair share of near campus real estate. There were two cars in the driveway – an apparently brand-new Fiat and a Land Rover.

'Anybody know what Mrs Fuchs does for a living?' I asked.

'We should have asked Dave,' Miranda whispered from the back seat.

'Call him,' Luna said.

'Jeez, not again,' my son said.

'Don't put it on speaker and I'll stay out of it,' I said.

'Thanks so much, Mother. It's really thoughtful of you not to openly flirt with a man half your age in front of your son. I mean, really, Mom.'

Sarcasm doesn't fall far from the tree.

'Whatever,' I said while he dialed.

'Dave. Pugh again. Listen, can you find out what Fuchs' wife does for a living?' Turning to the car in general, he said, 'What's his wife's name?'

'Annabelle,' Luna said.

'Annabelle Fuchs,' Graham said into the phone.

There were a few minutes of silence, at least in the car, while Dave did his thing. Then Graham began nodding his head and said, 'Yeah. OK, great. You know, thanks, Dave.' Then: 'No. And shut up.' Graham disconnected.

I grinned. 'Did he mention me?' I asked.

'Mother, I am telling Dad everything! Do you hear me? Everything!'

'Can it, you two!' Luna said. 'What did you find out?'

'According to their tax returns—'

'Jesus! That kid hacked the IRS?' Luna said, her face turning a pasty white.

'Whatever. Anyway, according to their tax returns, Annabelle Fuchs has had no income at all for the past five years.'

As a unit, we turned and looked at the beautiful Victorian on almost an acre of prime real estate. 'Nail number one,' Luna said.

Luna had started the engine and was about to pull away when a side door of the Victorian opened and Gaylord Fuchs came out carrying a small duffle bag, his much larger wife behind, loaded with suitcases.

'They know about Ng,' Luna said. 'And they're on the run.'

'So arrest them!' Graham said.

'It's not my jurisdiction!' Luna said.

'Follow them and we'll call it in to somebody,' I said.

She watched the couple start the Land Rover and begin to back out of the driveway. 'We're headed in the wrong direction,' she said.

'Then make a U-turn!' Graham said.

'They'll make us!' Luna said.

'So what? Follow them and, like Mom said, call it in!'

'To who? Champion's in the hospital—'

'Jesus, Elena, you want me to drive?' Graham said, unbuckling and leaning over the front seat as if he planned on joining us.

'Get back!' Luna said between clenched teeth. 'I've got this!' She pulled forward as they turned the opposite direction. 'Somebody write down the license plate.'

Miranda was furiously grabbing her phone and taking a picture of said plate. I never would have thought of that. I'd still be looking for a pen and paper.

To me, Luna said, 'Get hold of Champion in his hospital room. Find out who he wants me to call on this.'

'You don't know anybody else?' I asked, trying to figure out how to get the hospital's phone number.

'Would I ask you to do that if I did?' She was going to break a tooth the way her jaw was clenched.

Luna had made the U-turn and was hot on the Fuches' tail by the time I was put through to Champion's room.

'Champion,' he said on answering the phone, as if he was back in his cubicle at the police station.

'It's Pugh,' I said. 'The Fuches are running for it. We're on their tail but who do we call about this?'

'Fuck!' he said, and I could hear the rustle of bedclothes. 'I'm on my way! Where are you?'

'No!' I yelled. 'You're due in surgery in, what, an hour? Haven't they given you any meds by now? Jesus, Champion, try to think like an adult!'

'I've got to—'

'No! Just tell me who to call. Who in your department is up on this?'

'My captain. I've been reporting this to her. But don't you call her. Make Luna do it. The captain still thinks your son is our strongest suspect.'

'Then you haven't been reporting to her lately, have you?' I said, and if I sounded disgusted it was only because I was. Totally disgusted. 'What's her name and how do we get in touch with her?'

'Let me call her and she'll call Luna on her cell,' Champion said, his voice getting weaker.

'Her name?'

'Rios. Captain Sylvia Rios.'

'Call her now!' I demanded, hanging up, and relayed the conversation to Luna.

'Rios. Yeah. I know her. She was on that task force back in the day. She was a lieutenant then.'

'She's going to call you,' I said.

'Hope she hurries!' Luna said, taking a left turn into traffic, racing to keep up with the Fuches, who obviously knew they had a tail.

They were headed toward the IH 35 freeway, which was never a good thing. Although, in this case, it might be. Since IH 35 was a parking lot almost any time of day, it was a good bet one of us was going to be able to get out of the car and walk up to theirs. Maybe.

But Fuchs got to the turnoff to IH 35 and kept going into the east side of town. Although recent gentrification had begun, the east side was classically the poor side of Austin, and as such there was more crime and fewer police. The speed limit on the narrow streets was forty miles an hour; Gaylord Fuchs was hitting seventy and we weren't far behind.

I saw the big beach ball come flying off the sidewalk in front of Fuchs' car, followed quickly by a small boy. I screamed, Luna hit her brakes and Fuchs' car swerved, going out of control and landing upside down against a burned-out minivan. The little boy stood in the middle of the street, ball in hand, staring at the wreckage.

FOURTEEN

t hurt my ego a little, but Dave Wisher had gotten over me before I'd even left Austin. When told I was leaving, he simply said, 'Who?' Oh, well. Boys that age can be fickle, you know. Stuart Freeman sent us a bill that I thought far exceeded his involvement in the case but I was more than willing to pay it. Graham and Miranda are talking about getting an apartment off-campus. I'm keeping my mouth shut.

As for the players in the far from little test scam, they more or less got their just desserts. Gretchen Morley's very expensive attorney made a deal with the ADA and got her off with time served for rolling on Tina Ng. As far as I've heard, Tina Ng still hasn't said a word but Gaylord Fuchs is making up for her silence with an onslaught of information.

According to him, he and Ng had started the scam together since it was easy for Fuchs in his position to get hold of the tests. And it wasn't just economics class tests; he was able to get any test in the system and they were making money hand over fist – hundreds of thousands of dollars a year, apparently. Ng had brought Morley into it for her Greek contacts. Morley was selling tests to every fraternity and sorority associated with the university. Being the idiot she was, according to Fuchs, Morley had given a test to her then boyfriend, Bishop Alexander. Shortly after they broke up, Alexander demanded a cut or he'd go to the administration about the scam. Ng wouldn't make the deal on her own and said she had to talk to her partner. Although Morley didn't know of Fuchs' involvement, Alexander figured it out, went to a party at Fuchs' house and demanded his fair share, as he considered it. And his fair share, according to Fuchs, was to be eighty-five percent.

'That's when I took a swing at him,' Fuchs said, 'and missed.' He grinned sheepishly, as if having him killed had all been part of some elaborate joke. 'I mean, some of the kids told me he was saying mean things about my wife but obviously she didn't even hear it.' He shrugged. 'I wouldn't hit him for that. I know she can handle herself.'

It was Fuchs' claim that it was Tina Ng's idea to kill him, saying it was the only way to get him off their backs. Fuchs admitted she was right but said, 'I'm really not into that sort of thing. It just seems, you know, a little over the top. Even if Bishop Alexander deserved it more than most humans. If you could call him human.' His remorse, or lack thereof, wasn't going to go down well with a jury, Champion said.

Fuchs said he managed not to get involved in what happened, but did say that Ng convinced Morley to find a way to slip a roofie to 'the roommate,' so she, Ng, could get in and 'talk' to Bishop. Fuchs also said that Morley was stupid enough to believe that Ng was only going to 'talk.' After seeing Tina Ng in action on her takedown of Detective Champion, no one was surprised that she was able to subdue and kill a sleeping Bishop Alexander. Fuchs also claimed that his wife, Annabelle, knew nothing about the test scam or why he was leaving in such a hurry.

'She's a good woman,' Fuchs said. 'She does what I tell her to do.' He shook his head. 'I hope she finds someone new. Maybe someone who doesn't get himself in such hot water, you know?'

The college paper had a field day with the scandal and my son was named one of the primary people involved in taking down the ring. I'm sure he was more popular now with the faculty but maybe a little less so with his classmates, who had relied on the cheating scam. But better a reputation as a goody two shoes than as a murderer, am I right?

I got home in time to start on my bodice ripper that I planned on paying for a trip to Europe for two next fall. I obviously needed some alone time with my man.